# Legacy of Love

## A Romance Novel

by

Betty L. Killebrew

## DEDICATION

This novel is dedicated to my sisters, Ruth Alden and E. Jane Kelley, because they have always supported my efforts to be a writer by reading—and professing to love—everything I write.

# ACKNOWLEDGMENTS

Thank you to my long-deceased friend, Edna Nebeker, for allowing me, as a young woman, the chance to see the interior of her lovely home.

# CHAPTER 1

When Anne sank limply into the chair, the telephone slipped to the carpet at her feet. Shocked by her friend's reaction, Janet rushed across the room and knelt at her friend's side.

"What is it dear?" She questioned.

Anne simply whispered a name in answer, "Aunt Aggie..."

Janet knew intuitively, without further words, that Anne's beloved aunt was gone. She sank wearily to the floor alongside the sofa and began to pat the hand that trailed across her friend's shapely leg. This time Anne had been dealt a blow that really was too much.

For some time Janet continued to alternately stroke and pat the fine-boned hand that drooped listlessly toward the floor. She had never seen Anne so stricken and was reluctant to speak to her until she had come around to herself a little. Finally, though, the clock on the mantelpiece began to chime the hour. Six o'clock. One hour since Anne had arrived home radiantly beautiful and full of plans for the great adventure so near in her future. One short hour and all had changed.

With a sympathetic hand, Janet pushed the soft wing of auburn hair back from her friend's delicate cheek bone. "Come sit in the window, Love. I think it's time we both had a cup of tea."

"Time," Anne sighed. "If only Aunt Aggie had had a little more of it...And Papa too. Poor Papa. It's a mockery having the name of Long and having your life be so short."

"I know, love," Janet replied. "It's hard to accept such a thing. Nobody really understands why it should happen that way and especially to more than one in a family as it so often seems to." She linked her arm through the slender crook of the elbow of Anne Catherine Long and gently led her to the small round table in the bay window.

Janet Conard was greatly saddened by her friend's loss of a dearly beloved aunt, but she knew that now that Anne had begun to talk about it she would soon be all right. First she must get a cup of tea into her, eventually Anne would cry, and then the recovery could begin. But it was altogether too sad. Anne had simply lost too many of her loved ones—her mother in early childhood; two years ago her Papa; and now her last really close relative, Aunt Aggie. Janet's soft heart was breaking as surely as if it had been her own aunt whom she mourned.

Several days later when most of Anne's shock at Aunt Aggie's untimely death had been absorbed, the two girls once again took a cup of tea together in the little nook of the bay window.

"I feel so ashamed that I did not try harder to reach Aunt Aggie when she didn't answer my calls," Anne said. "I should have checked on her. I should have called *someone* in Fairfield to find out why she wasn't answering the phone. I was just going along the same as usual; she was dead and I didn't even know." Anne choked back a sob.

"No one could have known, Love," Janet soothed. "You know there have been other times when she was busy and you couldn't reach her for a while, but she was always fine. You couldn't know this time was different."

"I know that in my head, but my heart feels guilty," Anne replied.

Janet decided to change the subject. "Have you told them at your office that you won't be going to the States after all?"

Her friend shook her head. "I can't bring myself to say anything. If the rest of the staff started offering me sympathy over Aunt Aggie, I don't think I could stand it."

"But your notice will soon be worked out," her friend remarked with a worried frown. "Won't they be hiring your replacement soon?"

"They already have," Anne replied ruefully. "They gave the post to a really nice young lady. Fresh from secretarial training. I think she'll do very nicely."

"But what will you do?" Janet exclaimed.

"I suppose I will have to find another position," Anne sighed. "I haven't liked it that well with the two Mr. Garolds anyway; but up until now I had thought I would be leaving soon."

"Indeed, if you don't tell them shortly that you have no longer got a home to go to in the States you'll be leaving whether you want to or not. If you tell them straight away, I'm sure this new girl will be able to find another position easily enough. The schools do help place them when they finish their training, you know."

"No," Ann replied, this time with firmness. "I have made up my mind to leave the firm of Garold and Garold as planned. I have all the money I saved for the trip to the States. I need a change, and I'm sure something will turn up before I'm completely broke."

The phone call telling of her aunt's death had been made by a woman who spoke in a cool, businesslike, but not unkind voice on behalf of the law firm of Stevens and Green in the small community in New York State where Aunt Agatha had made her home since her marriage to Major Lester Brownfield. Anne was told that, in going over the effects of the late Agatha Brownfield, the firm had discovered evidence of her kinship to Anne Catherine Long of London, England and had felt that Miss Long would desire word of the death of her relative. Unfortunately, the relationship had not been discovered in time for Anne to travel to Fairfield for the funeral service. The caller expressed the firm's sympathy at her loss and promised a letter with details would be forthcoming, but it was clear the owner of the voice on the end of the line had no inkling that Anne would experience any sense of personal loss for an aunt who had lived and died so far away.

Although Anne's grief was increased by sorrow that her aunt had been gone for several days before she had known it, she knew that she could not have afforded to attend the funeral anyway. The only reason she had been able to save enough to move to the States was the fact that she would have been able to move in with Aunt Aggie and thus not have expenses until she was able to establish herself. She simply did not have the finances for flying half way around the world to a funeral, no matter how much it might have meant to her.

Anne had been in the United States several times before. She couldn't remember the first time, but she'd been back once when she was seven and again at the age of fourteen. She knew how helpful Americans could be, and she planned to ask the law firm's advice regarding a suitable marker for her aunt's grave. She also planned to wire some funds and ask the solicitor to place a wreathe on the grave in her name. That was something, at least, that she could do.

In spite of the distance between them, Aunt Aggie had been very close to her. Never having had children of her own, Aggie had warmed easily to the bright-haired, sad-eyed child her brother had sent her soon after the death of his wife. The next time Anne had come to the States it had been as if her own daughter had come home to Aggie.

The months of those two summers had sped by for the devoted aunt; and over the ensuing years Aggie had exchanged weekly letters with her niece and had phoned her the first Sunday of every month as well as on holidays and other special occasions. Photos and gifts had been sent back and forth regularly, and Aggie had visited London at the time of her brother's brief illness and death as well as on one other occasion for a long visit.

Recently, when Aggie had learned that Anne had finally decided to come to the States to live with her permanently, she had been elated. So elated in fact that her bad heart was likely given its fatal overload by the flurry of activity on which she embarked to make ready for Anne's arrival. Her heart would have broken much sooner had she known that her niece had avoided coming before with excuses made only because she was determined to earn the necessary money herself before making the trip.

When the promised letter arrived from the firm of Stevens and Green, the cream parchment was almost more than Anne could stand to touch because it brought her back to the moment she had received the fateful phone call. She stared at the U.S. postage stamp in the upper right and the unusual blue ink in script type which spelled out her name on the front. Finally, after several minutes, she almost ceremoniously slit the envelope with a seldom-used decorative letter opener. She slit it gently, reluctantly, although she knew that its contents would not have the power to affect her as strongly as the phone call had done.

She began to read, expecting the dutifully transmitted details of the lonely funeral of a woman who had died in a distant country. Instead, she discovered she was an heiress.

"Not a really large amount," the letter stated, "but a fine, well-kept old home built of a quality that could no longer be matched. The balance of her aunt's income had been an annuity that ended with her death, but Anne was also to inherit a small bank account and a five-year old automobile. "Among the furnishings," the letter continued, "some really fine antiques." It was suggested that she contact her own firm of solicitors and have them write to Stevens and Green regarding the details of the sale of the estate and the transfer to Miss Long of the money so obtained. A buyer had apparently already been found for the house, a buyer who would also be willing to purchase most of the beautiful old furnishings. All Miss Long need do was provide her "power of attorney, wait a bit," and the money would be delivered to her. Her solicitor could prepare the papers and she would need only to sign them.

"No," Anne said aloud. She left the rest of her small pile of mail on the desk top and hurried down the hall. "Janet, Janet," she called. "Janet, come here. I'm going to the States after all!"

# CHAPTER 2

"Promise you'll come over and see me for a long vacation sometime soon," Anne told Janet over and over in the days remaining before her departure.

"And promise me you'll come back some day, at least for a visit if not for good." her friend returned. "I'm not going to let your half of the flat, you know. If you do come back it will be waiting for you, and if you don't..." she shrugged, "Maybe Jeffrey will decide to pop the question and we could stay on here a bit."

"You're a dear," Anne told her, "But don't keep my room open for me if you find someone suitable to take it. I won't be coming back."

As the date of her departure grew closer the days sped by for Anne. Although she had no close relatives to tell good-bye, she had school friends, work friends, and those in her old neighborhood and in the new one where she and Janet shared their flat. It was necessary to say "good-bye" to all of those and also to say good-bye to her old way of life. She walked the streets of London one last time, looking at the familiar landmarks as she passed by. It was not likely she would ever come back to live here again. Brief visits, if finances fared well enough, were all she could expect to have of London in the future. Somehow, though, the fact that she remembered only two short summers in the United States notwithstanding, Anne did not feel that her trip to that destination was leaving home—she felt she was going home.

It was with that attitude that she gave Janet a final farewell hug and climbed aboard the transatlantic jetliner for the pre-dawn flight which would take her to the United States where she would be well and truly on her own.

It wasn't till after the plane was in flight that she first realized that on this third journey to the other side of the world she would, for the first time, not find Aunt Aggie there to greet the plane. Unaccountably this fact, which she should have realized all along, now made her begin to cry. Anne saw her last view of her homeland through a blur of tears; but she soon resolutely wiped them away with a clean handkerchief and sat up straight to enjoy the flight.

Within a short while the flight attendants had given the passengers a thorough briefing in the use of oxygen masks and in evacuation techniques should the plane be downed. Although a slight chill passed through Anne when the demonstration began, it was presented in such a matter-of-fact manner that she found herself listening with interest and with little fear.

Before she knew it, the demonstration was over and she was served a light breakfast of juice, hot tea, and a roll. After consuming the meal she felt able to square her emotional shoulders as well as her physical ones. It would never do to dwell on what might have been. Her entire future was before her and she knew it was up to her alone to make it a good one.

For a while after breakfasting Anne amused herself by looking out the window although there was little to be seen except the blue sky and the greenish-blue ocean with an occasional feathery, white cloud appearing either above or below the plane. The view, although beautiful, soon became monotonous.

She had brought a book along but was unable to concentrate on reading it, and her attention was soon captured by the antics of a small blond boy who was traveling along with his mother and a tiny infant girl. Observing that the woman had her hands full, Anne offered help and soon found herself cuddling the child on her lap as she read to him from a favorite story book while his mother cared for the infant. It was delightful to hold him and inhale his little-boy smell as she read, and Anne was surprised at the rush of love she felt toward a child she was seeing for only the first time. However, when the story was completed, he slipped immediately off her lap and gravely thanked her before returning to his own seat and curling up against his mother for a nap.

Anne felt an inexplicable longing as the little boy walked away. She found herself wondering if perhaps she would one day have a child of her own.

"Not likely," she thought. "I will probably be far too busy scrambling around trying to make a living to have time to look for a husband." Even more important, she realized, was the fact that, in spite of many dates with young men who were very interested in her, she had always failed to experience any spark of interest in return. She sighed. Perhaps she was destined to become an old maid. "Anyway," she said to herself, "At least I'll have a home."

As it neared the last hour of the flight, a second meal was served—a truly superb meal of chicken ladled with a light cream sauce and served with fluffy rice and tender asparagus, followed by a dessert of raspberry ice and crisp arrowroot biscuits. Fortified by the nourishing meal, Anne became impatient to end the journey and embark on her new life. She felt like cheering when she first sighted land through a break in the clouds below her and realized that the plane had begun to descend.

Although the other times Anne had traveled to the United States had been as a child, with airline personnel taking full responsibility for her care, she had no difficulty handling the transfer from the transatlantic flight to a commuter. After passing through customs, she simply asked the way and was given directions to her correct departure gate while her baggage was transferred by the airline.

Her troubles began when she reached the small city nearest the truly tiny community of Fairfield which was her destination. She watched her luggage being unloaded from the small commuter plane into a fenced compound. From there she saw it moved through a small door to an interior storage area. However, when she went forward to claim it at the desk, she was asked if her family had arrived to assist her yet.

"I thought you might just like to leave it here until they arrive," the girl on duty explained. "We don't have any baggage attendants in this small airport; and once we give you your baggage, you will have to take care of it yourself. If you just leave it here for now, I can get the boy from the back to go ahead and load it in your car when he brings it to the front."

"But nobody's coming for me!" Jenny exclaimed. "I planned to take a taxicab to the bus station. I hope there is a bus leaving for Fairfield this afternoon."

"There's no longer a bus service to Fairfield at all," the girl said, shaking her head. "It had so few customers they were forced to give it up about five years ago. If there's no one to come for you I guess it will have to be a taxi all the way. Would you like me to call one for you?"

"Yes, please do," Anne replied, grateful for the ever-present friendliness of Americans.

The arrangements for a taxi were soon completed although the airline clerk relayed to Anne the depressing news that the dispatcher had said it would be at least a half hour before any would be free. Anne, who was by now beginning to feel quite exhausted, accepted the information numbly and went in search of a cup of tea to help endure the wait.

She was soon reminded that she was 'home' in America when she was forced to settle for lukewarm coffee dribbled into a plastic container by an apathetic coin machine which only condescended to serve her at all after it had been fed twice the number of coins called for on its mirrored front—coins which Anne obtained from the ever-courteous clerk in exchange for a U.S. bill she had received that same day, quite early in the morning, in exchange for her native money.

She drank the coffee with no enthusiasm as she waited for the taxi. When it finally arrived, in more nearly an hour than in the half originally estimated, she was dismayed at the condition of the driver whom she discovered to be a wizened and wrinkled elderly gentleman with a distinct curvature of the spine. It seemed doubtful that he was capable of steering the large, yellow-checked cab from which he emerged. Anne, however, was in no mood to quibble. She claimed her baggage, and appreciated the assistance of the boy from the back with what she hoped was an adequate tip. It would have been impossible for her and the ancient driver to have handled the mountains of luggage on their own

Surprisingly, however, the old gentleman turned out to be quite a capable driver who handled the car smoothly and with self-assurance. It was well that he did, for Anne found herself quite appalled by the traffic which careened frantically along the highway, all seemingly on the wrong side of the road. It was well and good to know intellectually that drivers stay on the right side of the road in the United States. It was quite another thing to accept this strange behavior with equanimity.

She thought about the "five-year-old car" that awaited her in Fairfield. She hoped that the fact that she did not now drive would prove an advantage in learning to drive it. It seemed logical that driving on the right would prove easier for one who had never driven on the left—that is, if she could learn to drive it at all. She was certainly going to enroll in a good training school. One would need very good skills indeed to drive the same roads as these fool-hardy Americans!

Shortly, however, the highway gave way to a less-traveled roadway. And very shortly after that, Anne began to experience her first feelings of being in familiar territory. Although it had been many years since her last visit, she knew that this was a road she had ridden along a great many times with Uncle Les at the wheel and herself strapped in the back seat behind him and Aunt Aggie.

She smiled a little at the thought, and then the smile gave way in the face of the indisputable fact that both Uncle Les and Aunt Aggie were now gone forever.

Her sadness, though, could not endure for long. She was too excited by the fact that she would shortly be entering her own home for the first time in her life. Even when her father was alive, the homes they had occupied had always been rented. This would be the first time she would enter a house that was truly her own.

Thus she approached the beautiful little town, whose Presbyterian Church steeple stood like an exclamation point over the surrounding buildings, with quite mixed feelings. Indeed she was in a highly emotional state.

Her little old cab driver, possessed of an efficiency which belied his years, wheeled confidently into the first petro stop he came to and determined the location of the attorney's office she sought. He then wheeled her grandly to the front of a building along a deserted street which stretched emptily along for the two or three blocks which encompassed the business area of Fairfield.

It was then that she discovered an American small-town custom which was a surprise to her. The office was closed on Wednesday afternoons!

How foolish of her not to have more fully divulged her travel plans to the Stevens and Green firm when she had written, she thought, as she stood before the door reading the gilt letters which informed callers of the schedule of office hours. And why had she not waited for a reply to her letter before stupidly coming half way around the world to be greeted with nothing but a closed and barred office door? Without a key she would have no way of entering her Aunt's house. And actually, if she thought of it, she was not at all sure that she could remember where the house was; and she didn't have any idea of its address as she had always addressed her letters to Aunt Aggie via a post office box number. Anne burst into tears.

"There, there, little girl. What's the trouble?" The old cab driver stood beside her, pulling at his cap visor in embarrassment at witnessing her tears. Between sobs, Anne informed him of the situation as fully as she could as he stood listening with what she mistakenly took to be disgust on his face. "There, there little girl," he repeated, this time in a soothing voice. "I'll see what I can do."

With that, he disappeared; and Anne, deciding it was silly to stand crying on the street—albeit a deserted street—opted to get back into the cab to cry there instead.

After only a few minutes, in which she had not yet gotten around to drying her eyes, the light in the cab was suddenly darkened. Anne looked up to discover the light blocked by square shoulders comfortably clad in a buff jacket of a light-weight woolen worsted material. A warm chuckle from the wearer of the jacket caused her to look higher, whereupon her vision was instantly captured by blue eyes of such depth and clarity that they seemed an extension of the endless blue sky that she had so recently been privileged to view from far above the Atlantic Ocean.

"Miss Long, I presume," he commented in warm golden tones which were a fair match for his equally warm golden tan. He opened the door of the cab and stretched out a hand to assist her.

"Yes, I am," she quavered, as she belatedly dabbed at her eyes with a pocket tissue which had seen a little bit too much use already. An immaculate monogrammed handkerchief was immediately thrust into her hand in its stead; and as she accepted it, she felt a sharp thudding of her heart as her fingertips brushed against the strong, sinewy hands of the man who towered above her petite frame.

"Well, I'm Matt Stevens," he said matter-of-factly. "What are you bawling about?"

"The law office is closed," Anne wailed.

"Well then, I'll open it up again, if you'll just calm down," he replied with a shake of his unruly golden head.

Anne, mesmerized by this extremely attractive man who exuded vitality, was totally unable to collect herself and failed to grasp his meaning.

"How will I ever get into Aunt Aggie's house if the law office is closed on Wednesday?" she sobbed.

"I told you I would open it." This time there was a little additional stress on the "I."

"But then you must be…"

"Yes, I must; that's what I just said. I'm Matt Stevens a partner in this firm." He gestured at the early-American colonial brick facade of Stevens and Green.

"But you're closed," Anne persisted.

"Not anymore," Matt sighed. "I was enjoying an afternoon off; but, lucky for you, I was still in the cafe across the street when this gentleman came asking for me." He motioned with his hand toward the elderly cab driver who stood a few feet away, cap in hand, looking inordinately pleased with himself.

# CHAPTER 3

"I didn't think," Anne confessed, dabbing at her eyes with Stevens' handkerchief. She was uncomfortably aware that her blush was coming off her cheeks along with the tears. She tried a smile, "I'm sorry to interrupt your lunch."

"No problem," he answered. "I had finished—I was waiting for my little girl. She's rather slow."

Anne was struck by the mention of the child. Of course he would be married, she thought. She really ought to have known. How could someone as attractive as he have escaped? She turned away, hoping he would not notice her momentary reaction, and discovered that the cab driver was unloading her bags to the sidewalk.

"Oh, no!" she exclaimed. "I'm not staying here. I only came for a key. Leave everything in the car and wait for me."

But Stevens was already drawing his wallet from his hip pocket. "Never mind that," he said. "I'll see she gets where she's going. Will this do?" He handed the cabby a folded bill that caused the wrinkled old face to light up in a smile that exposed the loss of several teeth. A wizened, brown hand tipped the visored cap; and with a slam of the trunk compartment, the cab driver climbed into his car and was gone, leaving Anne alone on the street with Matthew Stevens who fished around in his pocket for a key, then unlocked the door of the building and began to carry Anne's numerous suitcases into the office foyer. No sooner was the job completed than a tiny, elfin girl pushed opened the door and peeked shyly around it toward Anne.

"Are you a client or can I come in?" she questioned forthrightly.

"Oh, no," replied Anne. "I mean, I suppose I am a client; but you can certainly come in anyway," she continued.

The tiny blonde head flew negatively from side to side. "Oh no, Daddy says I mustn't bother when he's with a client."

"Come in, Cupcake," Matthew said. "This is Anne Catherine Long from London, England. She is a client and you are bothering us, but I'm sure she'll forgive you.

"Miss Long, May I present my daughter, Karen. Karen, are you hiding something behind your back?"

The child nodded her head slowly.

"Show it to me."

The small hand slowly came round. In it was clutched a circular lollipop as big as the tiny face gazing upward. "Stella gave it to me."

"Stella had no business giving it to you. What's more, you had no business taking it."

"Do I have to take it back?"

"No, but you must save it for later. I can't have you eating that sticky stuff in the office or the car. You can eat it next time you go to the pool."

"You keep it for me," said the little girl. She handed the lolly to her father who shoved it in his coat pocket, leaving a large portion of it peeping out at a rakish angle. To cover her smile, Anne bent over and began arranging her bags neatly along the walls.

"Pick out whatever you'll need tonight," Matthew told her. "My car's too small to take it all over at once. Tomorrow I'll bring it over in my partner's car. His is much bigger."

So Anne chose two smallish bags to take with her and followed Matthew and the skipping little girl through the building and out the rear door to a graveled lot alongside the alley where a tiny, bright-red sports car was parked.

Karen immediately climbed into the front seat but was removed by her father so that Anne might sit in the bucket seat beside him. The little girl was relegated to her booster seat in

15

the somewhat abbreviated back seat and admonished to buckle her seat belt. Her father tossed the luggage into the vacant spot beside the little girl before sliding into the driver's seat.

"I'd really rather sit in front with my Daddy," Karen was heard to mutter before a stern glance from her father silenced her.

The tiny car pulled smoothly away from its parking place; and although the short drive to their destination included only the streets of the small town, Anne sensed that the vehicle had a powerful engine that, although tightly controlled by Matthew Stevens for in-town driving, was capable of carrying the car at great speeds if he chose to allow it to do so.

Anne did not, however, have long to contemplate the car's engine; for very shortly she found herself being wheeled into the crescent shaped drive of her new home. As she approached the side door where she would enter the house again and where she had entered it so many times in the past, she could almost see Aunt Aggie there waving her welcome. She wished desperately that she had come here the previous year as Aunt Aggie had begged. But she reminded herself that one must always live in the present. The past could not be changed. One could only learn from it.

She climbed from the car and helped Karen out also; then walked round to the baggage compartment at the rear of the car to where Matthew was unloading her cases. She did not look toward the door, for she found she was in no hurry to enter the house. She first wanted to make sure that she could control her emotions in front of this dazzling man and, more importantly, around the tiny, innocent child who was his daughter.

Eventually though, Anne could delay no longer and was forced to join Matthew Stevens under the small arched roof which covered the doorway. After a moment's fiddling with the key, the door swung open and Anne found herself standing in the landing of a narrowish stairway. *Down* led to the murky blackness of the cellar. *Up* led only a few steps to the cheerful old-fashioned kitchen. Anne passed in front of Matthew as he held the door open. She started up the stairs but, at the last moment, turned and reached for Karen's hand, ostensibly to help the child up the stairway but in reality because it felt better to be leading the little girl into the house than to enter it all alone.

Once inside, however, Karen soon bolted away from her and ran through the kitchen pushing aside the swinging doors and dashing forward into what Anne remembered was the main hallway of the house.

"I'm going to climb the stairs," she called back over her shoulder.

"Sorry," her father shrugged. "It's the circular staircase. She just loves it. She must run upstairs every time she comes. It's sort of a ritual with her."

"But how does she know the house?" exclaimed Anne, unable to keep the surprise from her voice.

"I've had her here on many occasions lately. We were...er... doing some work...; that is the firm was doing some work for Agatha before her death."

"I see," replied Anne. But she did not see at all. Whatever could Aunt Aggie have needed a law firm for?

"Well, now," Matthew Stevens said, rubbing his hands together briskly, "Let's get busy and check the house over. We've had the utilities turned back on since we heard you were coming; so if everything is okay, Karen and I can get out of your way."

"I'm sure it's quite okay," Anne said stiffly. The loneliness of the house without Aggie in it had begun to penetrate to her very bones, and she could barely trust her voice.

"Well then, I'll just get Karen and be gone," said Matthew speculatively. "I'll be back with your luggage in the morning, and if you have any problems we can look into them then."

"Oh, yes, and I owe you for the taxi bill. Perhaps you could show me how much. I am really quite stupid about American dollars."

17

"Let it go for now," Matthew growled. "I'll tack it on to the estate fee."

All too soon, he and Karen were gone. Anne instantly wished she had taken him up on his offer to check over the house with her. It seemed an unbearable thought that she must now go through it alone and must be all alone with the indisputable fact that Aunt Aggie was no more to be found in these fondly recalled rooms. With some uncertainty, she pushed open the door to the hallway and began her tour.

# CHAPTER 4

An hour later, having walked listlessly through all of the rooms and having gone through the first inevitable tears which had overcome her at the moment she entered her aunt's room where much of Aggie's personality seemed to remain, she pulled herself together and returned to the kitchen to inspect the cupboards to see what foodstuffs might have endured over the time which had elapsed since her aunt passed away.

She found tea, flour, sugar and other staples in amazingly large quantities, which was not surprising as she recalled from her earlier visits that Aunt Aggie kept an amazingly well-stocked larder. She was pleasantly surprised to discover that the refrigerator had been thoroughly cleaned of perishables, leaving only condiments and jellies and other such items which could last for a long time without spoiling. She wondered briefly who had been responsible for the cleaning job. Then she lifted a memo pad from its cup hook on the side of a cabinet and began her grocery list.

She soon slipped out of the house and down the walk to seek out the location several blocks away where she recalled having been sent as a child to purchase small food items for her aunt. Here though, an unpleasant surprise greeted her, for the business was closed up with the appearance of having been closed for quite some time. In fact, starched curtains, criss-crossed at the large front windows, gave every indication that the old corner grocery was currently being used as a dwelling place. She stood irresolutely on the sidewalk in front of the building for a few minutes as if Mr. Bello of her memories might suddenly materialize in the starched white apron she recalled.

And then amazingly that very thing happened, or near enough at any rate. Mr. Bello, a little older but otherwise not much changed, emerged from the door of the shop-house and spoke to her.

"Can I help you, Miss?" he asked.

"No, I wanted to buy something but I see the store has gone."

"Hey, I think I know you. You're the Brownfield kid, ain't you?"

Anne smiled broadly. "No, I'm Anne Long, but I am related to the Brownfields. Agatha was my aunt. How did you ever remember?"

Mr. Bello scratched his thinning but still curly hair. "Are you kidding? It's the accent. We don't hear too many such as that around here. Even your aunt Agatha had pert nigh lost it all in recent years. I sure do remember you. When you came into my store as a little girl I could scarcely understand what you was wanting when you asked me for some tea." He pronounced the word in an exaggerated fashion to rhyme with *way*. "You do some better now, though. I can understand you."

"It's nice to see you again," Anne ventured. She noticed Mr. Bello tilt his head slightly to listen more closely to her accent.

"You here to sell Agatha's place?"

"No, I'm here to live in it. Can you tell me where I can go to buy some groceries?"

"Well, to tell you the truth, there's nowhere these days but the supermarket. It's quite a piece. I doubt if you could walk it. Mrs. Bello needs a few things too, though; so you might come along with us as soon as she's ready. You sit right here on the swing while I go get her.

"Mama, Mama," he called. "We've got company." Then he bustled off to find his cheerful, plump little wife.

Anne accompanied the two to the supermarket; but from the few items purchased, she suspected that the trip had been made primarily for her benefit. It was not the time of day people such as the Bellos probably would have chosen for shopping. Despite his retirement, Mr. Bello seemed as energetic as ever; and Anne believed that if ever groceries were actually needed they would have been purchased much earlier in the day.

It was past dusk when the Bellos returned her to the side door of her house; and Anne experienced the guilty feeling that she had kept them from having their evening meal.

It was too late now, but in the morning she had better get down to business and find some sort of transportation for herself.

Tired from her hard day, Anne made her supper a simple meal of a cup of tea and fresh toasted bread and jam, some of which she devoured even as she went to and fro in the kitchen putting away her parcels. Before she had finished, she was startled by the sound of the antique door knocker, banging not at the side door she was accustomed to using, but at the front door at the far end of the hall. It had grown quite dark in the time she had spent in the kitchen so she was forced to fumble around until she found the light switch, which flooded the hall with brightness. She then went a little timidly forward to answer the door.

"I came over a little while ago to take you to dinner and you weren't here. I was worried about you."

It was Matthew Stevens standing in the doorway and Anne felt herself immeasurably lightened by his presence. With an effort to overcome what she feared was obvious jubilance; she took him into the long living room where she seated herself on an antique sofa while he walked around looking at the various decorative items with his hands in his pockets.

In spite of her illicit joy in the visit from the handsome man, whom she was certain was married, she was immeasurably weary. Her day, having started in the wee hours, had been spent chasing the sun; so that by now, although it was only evening here, it was far gone into the wee hours of the next day in the time zone to which she was accustomed. As she watched Matthew Stevens wander about the room, she allowed her head to lean back against

21

the comfortable upholstery as she did her best to converse with him.

"I'm glad to hear you were able to get along all right," he said with his back to her. "I really should have arranged to take you for a meal earlier, but I had Karen on my mind then and I really hadn't thought that there might not be any food here or anything. I don't want to stay now because I know you're tired, but we need to have a business meeting real soon."

Matt had turned around to gaze full on at the English girl as he talked. He stopped in mid-sentence as he felt an unfamiliar dipping sensation in his belly.

Anne Catherine Long was sound asleep. A wave of bright auburn hair lay across her incredibly fragile jaw which was also brushed by the silken fringe of her eyelashes. She had turned a little to one side so that her head was cradled in the corner of the sofa between its back and one of its wide high arms. She looked very vulnerable.

A few minutes later Matt carefully set the door to lock of its own accord when he left the house.

# CHAPTER 5

Full daylight had flooded through the living room before Anne awakened the following morning. She discovered that someone had removed her shoes from her feet, covered her with a knitted coverlet, and slipped a pillow under her head. She blushed as she realized it could only have been Matthew Stevens who had performed those intimate courtesies for her.

With the realization came double shame that she had fallen asleep while her caller was still there and also that her feeling of happiness at his arrival the previous evening had been so inappropriate in the light of the fact that he was a married man. His kindness, which had so heartened her the night before, was no doubt simply a part of his job as estate attorney. Perhaps there would even be an additional item tacked on his final bill to cover the duty of acquainting her with the house and the community.

Anne resolutely pushed thoughts of Matthew Stevens out of her head and went into the kitchen to make a hearty breakfast.

It was not much later when Anne pushed open the door to the carriage house-become-garage in order to look for something, despite the fact she had little doubt it was long gone. She was quite surprised upon entering to find that half the interior space was taken over by stacks of new lumber, carpeting, and plumbing supplies. She had not known any construction was going on in her aunt's home, and at first she could not imagine what the materials might be for. Then she realized that a sturdy staircase had been built to replace the loft ladder with its bottom end coming out barely six feet from the small side door of the carriage house. The construction must be taking place on the upper floor of the carriage house, which was, in Anne's memory, little more than an attic or loft which was seldom used. Before she could go up the stairs to check out the surprising development, however, Anne was startled by a voice from behind her.

"You must be Anne Long."

"Yes, it's I. How do you know my name?"

"I've been doing some work for your aunt here, as you can no doubt see. I've been wondering what was going to become of the project now. When I heard you had arrived I came right over to discuss it with you. My name is Bill Rodgers. My folks lived a few houses down, but they've moved to Florida now. Maybe you remember them, though. I believe your aunt and my mother used to be in the same bridge club."

"I'm sorry," Anne said. "When I came to visit my aunt she always dropped out of her bridge club for a while. She said she could play bridge anytime but could only mother me for a short time.

"What is it that you were doing here anyway?" she asked the attractive young man she found herself facing.

"We were turning the attic there into an apartment. I was staying with your aunt for a while, but I would have lived here if we had gotten it finished. It was a good investment for both of us. I was planning to have an inexpensive place to live while I go back to college, and your aunt thought the rent would be a fine aid to her finances in the future. She put up the money and I put up the labor." He shrugged his shoulders. "When Agatha passed away I moved out right away, of course. I've been staying at my sister's over on Maple Road a couple of houses down from the Bello's place. Mr. Bello came by this morning to tell me you arrived yesterday.

"Before this conversation goes any further," he continued, "I want to offer you condolences on losing your aunt. It's a great shame. She was a fine woman. She never stopped caring and being involved with other people. She'll be missed around here."

"Thank you," Anne murmured, blinking back tears.

"She was looking forward to your arrival so much. I know it must be hard for you to come here now that she's gone; but I assure you that's exactly what she would have wanted you to do," Bill continued sympathetically.

"As soon as she heard you had agreed to cone here she began to remake all her plans. She told me that she'd never prevent me from living here in the apartment but that she doubted she'd ever rent it to anyone else. I took it she had her heart set on you living in the house and raising a family there with her spending her last years here in the apartment. She told me I had better do a very good job of building it because she expected to use it for a long time. I sure wish she could have," he concluded with another rueful shake of his head. "We never know, though, do we?"

"Aunt Aggie used to say one should live as if we may die tomorrow and plan as if we would live forever," Anne told him. "I can see that she lived by her philosophy."

Anne found herself warmly liking Bill Rodgers. It was too bad that she would be unable to continue the arrangement with him. She, too, would no doubt have good use for the added income of a rental flat. However, she had no money at her disposal to continue the renovation.

"I'm sorry that you've been to so much trouble and spent so much time on this," she apologized "I would go along with the arrangement if I could, but," she shrugged, "I don't have a position as yet and I have no idea how long it will take to get one. My finances are very limited. I could not afford the things you'll need to finish, so I will almost certainly have to let this project rest for the time being."

"Have you been upstairs yet?" Bill questioned.

She shook her head. "I've only just this minute walked in the door. I was looking to see if my old bicycle was still here. I'm going to need transportation to do my marketing until I am able to arrange for driving lessons."

"Come on upstairs first," Bill told her. "You might be surprised."

He followed closely behind her as she climbed the short staircase and leaned around her to push the door open. Although the door was neither stained nor painted—it was raw new wood—it opened smoothly on its new, freshly-oiled hinges. Inside, Anne was indeed surprised. The apartment was actually almost finished.

"See," he told her. "The materials have all been purchased already. All that remains is for me to finish the work. You can have all the time you want to make up your mind, but I hope you'll let me continue." He grinned a slightly off-center grin. "I've already got a lot of myself invested in this place and I've been looking forward to living here."

"But, I don't understand," Ann said. "From the size of the stack of lumber below, I thought you were only just beginning."

"Oh, that!" Bill laughed. "Your aunt was so enthusiastic about this project that she ordered all the lumber, paint, and plumbing supplies before I could even begin." He smiled broadly.

"At first we could hardly even get inside. I had to use up the lumber as quickly as possible just to give myself room to work. Don't worry about the pile downstairs, though. I'm still going to use some of it, and Abbott's Lumber Yard will give you credit for whatever you don't use. They understood your Aunt Aggie. You might even come out ahead."

"Well, then," Anne said thankfully, with only the absolutely necessary amount of reservation. "I expect it will be all right. I will have to check it with Aunt Aggie's attorney, though. At least until I officially take possession through the—what do you call it here—Probate court?"

At that comment, Anne thought she saw a slight grimace pass over Bill Rodger's face; but she soon forgot about it as she began to explore the three rooms which were, in spite of their small size, remarkably attractively proportioned. On one side of the largest room the rounded eaves gave way near the top to a skylight. Bill caught the direction of her gaze. "A southern exposure," he explained. "It not only provides lots of light but should help keep me warm as well."

Anne pushed away a panicky thought regarding how she would keep warm in the main house, which must surely burn gallons and gallons of oil during the cold New England winters. She resolutely turned her full attention to the plans for completing the painting and decorating of the flat.

Later, Bill showed her where he had contrived storage space for her aged bicycle by hanging it from the rafters in what once had been the tack room off the main room below. That small room also contained many supplies for the new flat, including paint and stacks of cartons containing tiles for the bathroom and tiny kitchen area. With difficulty Bill extracted the bike and wheeled it through the narrow walking space into the sunlight. It creaked ominously and the tires appeared to be completely ruined, the rubber being dry and almost scaly, with cracks here and there.

"Oh, dear," said Anne, "I hardly think I will be able to ride this."

"Don't worry," Bill told her. "Give me a day or so and I'll get it going for you; and I have an old truck," he nodded toward the rear driveway, "and I'll be happy to give you a lift when you need to go somewhere."

"And I, too, will be happy to assist you, Miss Long."

Anne's heart missed half a beat as footsteps approached from the other side of the house. As she turned toward the newcomer, she felt a change in Bill's attitude, a sort of stiffening.

"I'll take the bike with me and bring it back when I have it fixed," Bill said gruffly. Then he was gone, leaving Anne standing alone in the sunshine and light breeze with Matthew Stevens.

# CHAPTER 6

"I've brought your luggage," Matthew said pleasantly, but his eyes were on Bill Rodgers' departing truck and his expression did not match his pleasant tone, "and I need to unload it right away. I'm on my way to court for what should be a very short hearing. I'd like you to have lunch with me later, if you would; and afterward, we can discuss your aunt's estate. I've been appointed executor, but as you are the primary heiress, you should know exactly how things are being handled."

"Of course," Anne replied carefully. "I'll be happy to come to your office whenever it's convenient for you. There are some things I really need to know; but," she continued, "I don't expect you to take me to lunch. I don't want to be a burden to you."

"I want to take you to lunch," Matthew interrupted. "Not as a duty—just because I want to get to know you better. Now, is it settled?"

Anne decided quickly "As long as I'm not being an imposition on you," she replied, and even though he was a married man, added to herself, "I certainly won't mind!"

"By the way, your aunt did have a car, you know," Matthew reminded her. "Recently she had to leave it sitting in the driveway because of the piles of lumber in the garage; so after she died, I put it in the garage down at our office to keep it out of the weather. I'll bring it over to you, if you like. You'll be able to use it as soon as I get the title changed to your name and you buy the license plates."

"I won't need it for a while," Anne told him. "I don't know how to drive, but as soon as I get organized I intend to learn. By then, maybe the garage will be cleaned out so I'll have a place to keep the car."

"No problem," he said. "I'll keep it as long as you like. Stop in sometime and look it over. Right now I'll get that luggage unloaded; then I have to run. I'll be here to get you about one o'clock, okay?"

Anne agreed to be ready at one and returned to the house with Matthew Stevens to help him unload her luggage, but he insisted on doing the lifting himself. He had parked a large, dark-gray sedan near the front door and also insisted, after bringing the bags through that door, on carrying them up the tricky circular staircase as well. He left them in the broad hallway of the second floor before hurrying away to avoid being late for his court appointment.

Anne spent the remaining time before lunch unpacking her belongings and hanging them in the closet of the same room she had used as a child. The crisp, freshly-washed curtains and a cheerful new counterpane on the bed gave evidence that her aunt had already completed most of the preparations for Anne's arrival before her untimely death. Anne knew she would never take this room for granted. It harbored a comfortable feeling of welcome for her, along with a tinge of sorrowful nostalgia for her aunt. As she unpacked in the comfortable nest her aunt had prepared, she knew that although someday she might change other things in the house, she would want this room to always remain the same, the way Aunt Aggie had planned it to be for her arrival.

Since she had been limited in what she could bring to her new home on a transatlantic flight, Anne had brought few accessories with her; so once her own things were put away, she crossed to her aunt's room to see if there was anything there which would augment her wardrobe. Many of the clothes that had belonged to the older woman were not suitable for one so young as Anne, but all of the items were conservative and of good quality, and there were some things that Anne knew she would find really useful when she could bring herself to wear them.

For now, she chose from her aunt's closet only a navy blue leather belt to wear with her own navy blue skirt and white polyester 'silk-look' blouse.

Ready in advance of the time Matthew had set, she settled in the cool shade of the deep front porch to watch for his arrival. Across the paved but seldom used road which fronted her house was a deep fertile field which ended in a line of trees which she knew edged the small river which formed the east boundary of Fairfield. Probably the river was the reason that years ago the town of Fairfield had been established at this location.

The view was spectacular, but Anne recalled that it had been totally lost upon her on her two earlier visits. When she had tarried on this porch as a child, it had been to play at jacks on the smooth concrete. As a teen she had watched the fireworks burst brightly over the river on Independence Day; she had also sometimes sat on the porch and watched traffic on the road in front of the house; but she did not recall ever before realizing the beauty that surrounded her. No wonder Aunt Aggie had been content to make this small community the home of her heart. Anne could easily believe that someday she too would cease to feel the call of her native England if she could live forever in this beautiful, peaceful town.

Relaxing in the warmth of the summer day and admiring the verdant fields in her view, she nearly forgot that she was waiting for Matthew to arrive. It was the joyful leaping of her heart at the sight of his tiny car that reminded her. Later, when she thought of it again, she was sure she had felt the leaping of her heart a split second *before* he drove into sight.

So that's the way it is with me, she thought, as his car pulled into the drive. Millions of men in the world and I fall for a married one. But she pushed the thought from her head and gave herself up to the pleasure of seeing him. After all, she was just having a business meeting. She had not and would not do anything wrong. She might as well enjoy the moment. Her business with him would soon be over and then she would not be seeing him anymore.

"I hope you don't mind eating at the cafe in town," he said as he leaned over the seat and pushed the door open for her after she walked across the lawn to greet him. "It's not fancy, but there's a private room in the back. I often take clients there. It gives us a chance to have a good meal and then a private conversation about business matters without the bother of returning to the office."

"I'm sure it's quite nice," Anne heard herself say stiffly as her dream world deflated. It was quite one thing to know their meeting was strictly business and an entirely different thing to try to enjoy the pleasure of Matthew Stevens' company with him stressing the business nature of their meeting with every word. Maybe she would find a secretary in the 'private room' to take notes of their 'business meeting'.

"Stella, I'd like you to meet Anne Long, lately of London, England and currently of South River Road," he said to the beautiful, but brassy blonde who approached them immediately after they entered Stella's Cafe.

"How do you do," Anne murmured politely, but she stopped short of extending her hand to shake when the older woman made no move toward her.

"Can we have the little room?" Matthew asked. "We have some business to discuss after lunch."

Anne wondered if she really noticed Stella's eyebrows rise ever so slightly.

"His Honor, the mayor, is in there right now with some industrial types; but they've already been served dessert, so I'll check." She tossed her head in an unsuccessful attempt to control her irritation and turned away. Matthew's hand on her sleeve stopped her.

"Not necessary, here they are now." Several men in business suits were filing through a door in the rear.

"I'll get the table cleared," Stella said shortly and walked away with both hands shoved into the deep pockets of her bright strawberry colored uniform and her shoulders hunched forward defensively.

"Matthew, my boy," said a rotund gentleman with a rosy face above a startling tie of bright sea-green. "You should meet these gentlemen. They represent hope for Fairfield's future."

"Indeed I should," Matthew said cheerfully. "I've already been asked to represent several property owners in making a firm stand to protect our local zoning laws."

"Oh, ho, ho," the mayor chortled. "The townsfolk won't object to this project. These gentlemen are going to build a factory that looks like a hotel. It will be clean, attractive and will supply badly needed jobs."

"I certainly hope you're right, Mayor. Allow me to present Miss Long. She's living at the old Brownfield place." All of the gentlemen murmured polite acknowledgments to her introduction, after which the Mayor introduced his dinner companions to Matthew. One of the gentlemen looked familiar to Anne, but she failed to catch his name and assumed she was mistaken because, having just arrived in the country, she knew scarcely anyone.

After handshakes were exchanged, Matthew took Anne's elbow and escorted her to the private room where they were to lunch.

Stella was laying the table with silver. "I'll send Joanie in to wait on you," she said. She then flounced away. Matthew's eyes rested for a scant moment on the door that swung shut behind her. Hell hath no fury… he thought to himself; but the thought trailed off as he turned back to his beautiful, auburn-haired companion.

"Business can wait until after lunch," he said firmly; and he skillfully steered the conversation toward Anne, her life in the past, her hopes for the future, and why she had chosen to come to the United States. So carefully did he probe that Anne found herself answering all of his questions without realizing that she herself was discovering little about him. In truth, she felt she would be content to sit across from him and talk about whatever he wished for the rest of her life, so much was her pleasure in watching his expressive face react to everything she said.

Dinner was the day's special, hearty and tasty, followed by cheesecake with chocolate drizzle for dessert.

"It's refreshing to see a young woman who's not afraid to eat," Matthew remarked with a slight grin as she finished her cheesecake.

Weight had never been a problem for Anne and she usually ate with a hearty appetite. Just now, however, she wished she had not eaten with such gusto. Perhaps Matthew Stevens did not think it was quite ladylike for a girl to enjoy her food. She was glad to see that he was bending over to pick up his briefcase and had apparently missed the slight blush she could not suppress.

The details of Aggie's estate which Matthew laid before Anne were straightforward enough. She was shown the balance of the bank account, the small sum remaining from life insurance following the burial, and the tax statements from the house. Even though Anne knew little about American dollars, it was clear to her that the annual tax bill for her house would soon use up her meager inheritance. It was imperative for her to get a job. But Matthew, it seemed, had other plans for her future; and he wasted no time in telling her his thoughts on the matter.

"The best course for you to follow," he said evenly, "is for you to arrange to sell the house right away. It's too big for you and will simply eat up all of your inheritance. On the other hand, if you sell the house, it will bring a good sum. As I wrote you in London, I have a ready buyer so arrangements can be made at once. As soon as the details are out of the way, you can relax and have a nice vacation before you go back home."

Green eyes, across the table suddenly glared at him with vehemence. "Mr. Stevens," Anne said sharply. "I'm afraid you have very much mistaken me. I'm not here for a vacation. I'm not

33

here just to settle my aunt's estate. I intend to live here and the house is NOT for sale."

"I hope you know what you're doing," Matthew said soberly as he returned the papers to his briefcase. "A young girl like you with a big house like that, well..." He shook his head.

"Perhaps I'm not as helpless as you think," Anne said frostily, although in fact she had no idea how she would manage to keep her house.

"Well, give it a try anyway," Matt growled. "The buyer will probably wait a while. He's not interested in just any house. He wants that one." And although Matt seemed to be speaking to her through gritted teeth, at the same time Anne felt he meant to encourage her. Her brilliant smile was his ample reward for his half-hearted kindness.

The drive back to Anne's new home was a short one, a matter of only a half dozen blocks or so; but during the scant few minutes it took to reach their destination, a kind of tension seemed to develop between Matthew and Anne.

Anne found it difficult to keep her eyes turned discreetly out the car windows rather than gaze, as she wished to do, at the strong brown jaw of the man seated so near her in the tiny car. Glimpses of Matthew's hands resting lightly on the steering wheel were equally intriguing, for Anne had never seen any as attractive before—beautifully shaped, with fingers long, tapered and perfectly manicured, yet in no way effeminate, but rather seeming to combine strength with a gentleness which was apparent in the way he caressed the car's wheel. A shiver passed along her spine as she thought involuntarily of having those hands touch her.

It was perhaps because of the turning her own thoughts were taking that Anne momentarily thought that Matthew might kiss her when he turned toward her after parking the car in her driveway. Matthew was in fact sorely tempted. She was very near and he was extremely conscious of her beauty. The faint fragrance which defined her was maddening within the confines of the little car, but Matt did not act on his desire.

He could not kiss Anne Catherine Long. Not only was she a client, but she was not the kind of girl he could kiss and then walk away from. "But of course," he said aloud to himself later as he pulled his car back onto the road to return to town, "she just might be the girl I *wouldn't want* to walk away from."

# CHAPTER 7

"Do you mind if call you?" Matthew asked as he turned toward her, having successfully overcome the urge to kiss her luscious lips.

"I don't believe you can, Mr. Stevens," Anne laughed a little nervously. "I'm sure the phone's not on service."

"It's not right now," Matthew admitted, "But it will be later today. I've arranged to have it turned on. You can't live alone without a home phone in this valley. The cell service is too erratic; and by the way, call me Matt."

Before Anne got over her surprise at his peremptory manner, he was gone; and she had totally forgotten to tell him she could not accept social phone calls from married men.

The old pick-up truck parked in the rear drive and the sound of hammering gave evidence that Bill Rodgers was at work in the carriage house. Anne was just inserting her key in the lock when she heard him call to her. Looking up she saw that he was leaning from a window in the upper apartment.

"Come on over for a while," he called. "I could use a break."

"Let me change first," she answered. "If I put on some old clothes, maybe I can help."

In her aunt Aggie's room she found what she needed, a pair of worn but clean blue jeans that Aggie had probably worn for gardening. Although they were a little short of leg, they fit well enough because Aunt Aggie had been blessed throughout life with the same natural slimness which Anne had received as legacy from their ancestors. To the jeans, Anne added a jersey which she had brought to her new home even though it had seen better days because it was an old favorite. Shoving her feet into a pair of sneakers completed her outfit.

Before joining Bill, she stopped in the kitchen for a plate of biscuits—she'd have to remember to call them cookies now—and a tall glass of milk. She doubted Bill would be interested in drinking tea and she didn't want to take the time to prepare it anyway.

She left the house by the rear door, setting the cookies on the broad, white, freshly-painted porch rail to pull the door behind her; but when she reached the carriage house she found nowhere to set the food. With both hands full she was unable to open the door, so she kicked it lightly with her foot; and Bill Rodgers immediately opened it for her. Shoving his hammer into a loop of his tool belt, he took the cookies and milk from her as his widening eyes and a quick whistle of appreciation let her know he found her attractive.

"You sure do something for Aggie's jeans," he commented; and then, seeing her surprised expression, pointed to a tiny, white spot on Anne's right thigh and explained. "I recognize that little paint spatter right there. She wore those jeans when she painted the porch rail. She wanted everything to be perfect for you, you know."

"It would be perfect, too," Anne said, "if only she were here with me."

After a short break in which he ate cookies and drank his milk, she and Bill were soon working together as if they had been helping one another for years.

"I'm sure glad you were here to help," Bill told her as he placed the last screw in a diminutive wall cabinet he was installing in the kitchenette. "A fella can't hold one of these things up and fasten it at the same time. If you hadn't showed up I'd have had to wait until my brother-in-law could help me."

"I never knew carpentry could be so much fun," Anne commented, then added wryly, "I wonder if I could make my living at it."

"Quite a few women do these days," Bill answered; "But I don't quite see you in that light. What kind of work did you do in England?"

"Secretarial mainly, though I was called a management assistant; but I don't think I can make enough money that way to keep the house." She gestured toward the sturdy edifice visible through the open window. "Which reminds me, I have to warn you not to depend too thoroughly on living here. I may have to sell. It's what Matt thinks I should do."

"Matt?" he queried.

"Mr. Stevens, my aunt's attorney," Anne answered with a hint of embarrassment at having been caught calling her professional advisor by his first name. To cover the embarrassment, Anne soon found herself telling Bill about her lunch meeting.

"Did you meet Stella?"

"I did, but she didn't seem very friendly."

"She made a play for Matt a while back and didn't get anywhere. She probably thinks you're doing better," Bill told her.

"But isn't Matt married?" she exclaimed. "I mean, I met his little girl and thought...I guess I just assumed..."

"Of course, he was married once," Bill answered. "His wife was killed while Karen was still in diapers."

"Oh, no! How sad for the child," Anne said, but to her shame she felt joy at news of the other woman's death. *Matthew is free,* she thought. *He's free! He's free!*

But Anne's joy was tempered by the realization that if Matt had his way he would send her right back to England. He'd probably even help her pack her bags. "He wants me to leave," she thought; "and how can I stay here? How will I ever support this house?"

"Do you know where there's a driving school?" she asked Bill.

"There's none within fifty miles," he snorted in reply.

"Well then will you teach me to drive?" she asked him. "I'm going to have to learn if I'm going to get a job, and if I don't get a job right away I'll have to give in and sell the house to the *ready buyer* Matt keeps telling me about?"

"Sure," he said easily. "I'll teach you to drive as soon as you get a learner's permit; but I wonder, did Matt tell you who wants to buy the house?"

"I never even asked. I don't know anybody here anyway."

"Next time you see him," Bill told her slowly, "ask him." He then turned away and made himself very busy measuring the tiny counter top to mark the space where a hole would be cut for the sink.

A little later, after she helped Bill stow his tools away and clean up the mess created by the day's work, Anne returned to the house, but only after declining an invitation to take the evening meal with Bill in a neighboring city.

"Some other time," she said. "Right now, I want to spend a little time just being in the house. I want to soak up the essence of Aunt Aggie from the floors and the walls before it begins to fade."

But it was a bubble bath she was actually soaking in when she heard the phone ring. Wrapping herself in a towel, she went to answer it.

"I just called to give you your phone number," Matt told her, and was surprised to hear unrestrained laughter as a response.

"What's so funny?" he inquired.

"It's such a cliché," she replied. "The phone always rings when one is in the bath and then to hear you say you called to give *me* my phone number!"

"You, my dear, have gone giddy. I think you have jet lag."

"I suppose I do," she gasped between giggles.

"Go and rest," he said.

"I will," she promised, "Just as soon as you give me my phone number."

"Just look in the book," he told her. "Aggie's old number wasn't taken yet so I got it back for you. Now will you go and rest?"

"Of course," she said; and hung up the phone without any further words.

# CHAPTER 8

It was only after Anne had climbed into her bed and felt herself begin to drift toward much-needed sleep that she suddenly wondered why Bill did not appear to care much for Matt Stevens, but she did not pursue the thought. Instead she allowed herself to imagine riding in Matt's car once more, her eyes on his beautifully shaped hands. She imagined him turning toward her and gazing at her with his sky blue eyes, and she fell asleep with the beginning of a pleasant dream already formed.

Because she had gone to bed early, pink streaks of dawn were just appearing when she wakened the next morning, totally refreshed. She was glad she had left her drapes open enabling the light of the sun to awaken her, for the sight of it rising to the east just above the trees along the river was spectacular. She did not, however, tarry long to look at it. She had work to do.

After her breakfast, Anne walked through the house to take stock of what housework was required. Although everything was in perfect order as Aunt Aggie had always kept it, a thin film of dust had settled over everything. Since Anne planned to find employment as soon as possible, she knew she would need to have some kind of system in order to keep the work done. She decided that she would be able to keep up by thoroughly cleaning one room each day.

She began with the formal living room, which she recalled Aunt Aggie had held in great pride. It was fitted with rich old carpeting of burgundy colored wool with swirls of rose and green. The walls were nearly white with just the palest hint of green pigment in the paint, and the wide moldings and other woodwork were of fine golden oak. The best part, however, was the adjoining sun room, which extended from the side wall of the house—a fifteen-foot oval of glowing sunlight with a fine tiled floor and beautifully detailed, multi-paned windows extending floor to ceiling. Although the plants Aunt Aggie had prized were no longer in their places on the plant stands, they were still present in Anne's memory and she would replace them as soon as she could.

She remembered the round oak table in the center of the sun room as a perfect place to have tea and she stroked the tabletop lightly with her fingertips as she remembered Aunt Aggie treating her with tea and little cakes served on her finest china as she shared with that dear relative her most treasured inner thoughts.

But the work still needed to be done, so Ann broke off her reverie and fetched Aunt Aggie's ancient Hoover from a storage closet at the rear end of the long hall; and finding that it was still quite functional, soon vacuumed first the carpet and then the upholstered furniture, which consisted of graceful side chairs which stood to either side of the wide opening to the sun room; the old camel-backed, wood-trimmed sofa which stood across from the opening; and a deep, comfortable overstuffed chair where her uncle had often fallen asleep as he read his evening paper.

After she finished the vacuuming, she dusted each table and the wooden parts of the chairs with great care, finding the dusting to be hardly a chore, so much did she enjoy the feel of the finely crafted pieces. The entire house, but particularly this room, seemed to symbolize Aunt Aggie to her, for like its late mistress, the house, while no longer young, was still graceful; and while undeniably it possessed beauty, the beauty was secondary to its suitability to its purpose, much as Agatha had been beautiful in her quiet simplicity and devotion to duty. Although the prospect of caring for such a large house and providing for its upkeep was daunting, Anne could not conceive of having it pass out of her hands. Yet Matt Stevens' opinion, expressed at their luncheon, had concerned her more than she cared to admit. She wondered if she was up to the task she faced.

Well, she thought, if I'm going to keep this house, I can't just stay in it all the time. I'll have to learn to be a part of this community if I'm going to keep the house. She looked around the comfortable old room she had just cleaned and knew that she would keep it forever if she could; and if she could not keep it, she would truly *lose* it; she would not willingly let it go. And armed with that determination, she swiftly put away her cleaning tools and went upstairs to her bedroom to freshen up before making her first solitary foray into the community.

Dressed in pearl gray slacks with a crisp white blouse, her narrow waist banded by a slim belt, she stepped into a pair of comfortable, low-heeled shoes for her walk into town, a distance of only a mile or so. While the town was not large, she did not know where anything was located. It was possible she would do a good deal of walking before returning home.

The walk toward town took Anne past a number of homes which were larger and more stately than her own as well as a greater number which were more modest. Unlike homes in the city neighborhoods of London with which she was familiar, each dwelling was unique. Even the occasional houses which showed evidence of originally having been built from identical or similar plans had undergone alterations which made their current facades distinctly different. The homes were all well-kept and each had its own carefully trimmed grass lawn which ranged from that which Anne would have found large in her own crowded city to grassy areas which looked park-like to her eyes. Anne was delighted with what she saw and awed by the spaciousness that Americans seemed to take so much for granted.

She passed few people on her mid-morning walk, only a couple of small children; one middle-aged woman, walking in a brisk fashion as if for her health, and two elderly men. Each person she passed spoke a cheery hello to Anne and gave her a warm smile; and unbeknownst to her, each one stopped a few feet farther along to gaze back at the radiant stranger, for they seldom saw strangers in town, much less one of such beauty; and the precise, clipped accent with which she answered their greetings made her all the more intriguing.

Her first objective was the post office. While Aunt Aggie had received her mail at a post office box, Anne wanted to find out if she could have home delivery, which would be easier for her for the time being, since she had no transportation. She found the building easily, located as it was down just one block from the town square and marked by several postal boxes around its perimeter.

On inquiry, she learned that home delivery was indeed available everywhere in Fairfield; she need only buy a mailbox and have it installed and delivery could begin at once.

While at the post office, she made arrangements for any mail she received at General Delivery to be forwarded to her at her home, then departed to find a store where the box could be purchased, hoping that within a few days of installing it she would receive a hoped-for letter from Janet Conard. She missed her friend more than she had believed possible. After having shared a flat with Janet for several years, that young woman was like a sister to her, and was, in fact, now the nearest thing to family that she had.

When Anne emerged from the post office, it took only a little looking to locate a bank across the street. She was nearly out of U.S. cash, so she went to the bank to make financial arrangements. After a short conference regarding her needs, she filled out a form to open an interest-bearing checking account. Her initial deposit was nominal, consisting of the travelers' checques she had with her in her handbag. She would deposit the rest of the funds she had brought with her on her next trip to town; and with a bank account, she would be able to have the money she had left in London transferred to this country with no difficulty.

Upon leaving the bank, Anne soon found a hardware store on the town square with a miscellaneous assortment of goods in its front window. It looked like a likely place to purchase her mail box, and it turned out there were several types of boxes available. Anne chose the one which looked like it would be most at home when fastened to her dignified old house.

The young clerk who served her was most helpful in explaining how the box could be fastened up, even volunteering to come over and put it up for her if she wished; but Anne assured him that she would have assistance, as she assumed that Bill Rodgers would come to her aid. The young man "Call me Rick," he said eagerly, was visibly disappointed. However, he was immediately cheerful when he learned her address was near his own.

He offered to stop in sometime to see if she needed anything, reminding her that she would probably need help with her lawn. Anne agreed that she would need an introduction to the mysteries of her lawn mower, assuming that she had a lawn mower, and left the store in good spirits, wondering who had been caring for her beautifully-kept lawn since Aunt Aggie's death. Unused to lawn care as she was, she had not previously given the matter any thought.

She soon found herself passing the law firm of Stevens and Green and briefly considered stopping in to satisfy her curiosity about the lawn. While there, she could also have a look at Aunt Aggie's car as Matt had suggested; but with honest insight Anne realized that she was merely attempting to justify a stop at the law firm to satisfy her real desire which was to see Matt Stevens again; and so she continued down the road with her head held high and determinedly straight-forward, not trusting herself to even glance at the building whose occupant held such fascination for her.

With her eyes fixed firmly toward the front, she spotted ahead of her a painted wooden sign on a renovated colonial style building which rivaled the law firm with its attractive facade. "Fairfield Journal," stated the sign simply in script style lettering. Anne went inside to order newspaper delivery, reasoning to herself that she would not get a job unless she was able to peruse the help-wanted ads.

Once inside, she learned that the Fairfield Journal was a weekly paper printed only on Wednesdays; but she discovered that the Fairfield Journal was also agent for a large daily paper printed in a nearby city. She ordered delivery of both papers for the time being. Once she had a job she could give up whichever she liked the least in order to save money; but for now, she needed all the information that was available to facilitate her job search.

By now it was well past lunch time, and as Anne stepped out of the newspaper office she looked toward Stella's Cafe and briefly considered lunching there before returning home. As she hesitated, a car pulled up in front. Though she was nearly a block away, Anne easily recognized the woman emerging from the car by her bright blond hair and strawberry uniform. Even as Stella was still climbing from the car, Anne saw the opposite door swing open and a small, brown-haired pixie fly around the front of the car. The child would have run directly into the road had not Stella caught her by the arm and stopped her in mid-flight.

Anne watched as Karen danced impatiently beside Stella until a couple of cars had passed. Then Stella led the little girl across the road and both of them disappeared behind the heavy door of Stevens and Green, Attorneys-at-Law.

As Anne no longer felt hungry, she turned her steps toward home. For the return trip, however, she varied her route by turning to walk a couple of blocks west of the street she had formerly followed with the idea of seeing different scenery. As she walked south on the new street, not quite as affluent as the one she had followed on her trip toward town, she was able to see down a cross road to the supermarket she had visited with the Bellos. She decided to pay her second call at the Great Deal Food Store. There she made a few small purchases, notable among them a re-usable net ecology bag and a chocolate bar.

When she left the store a few minutes later, she shoved her handbag and the awkward sack containing the mailbox into the net bag and set off for home, the chocolate bar in one hand, the bag swinging from the other. As she trudged along, her thoughts turned inexorably toward Matt Stevens; and this time she did not try to turn them in another direction. With a sigh she bit into the thick, rich chocolate.

Some minutes later, after the candy bar had been consumed and the wrapper carefully stored in her net bag, a vehicle drew alongside her; but Anne was still so preoccupied with her thoughts that she was unaware of its presence until she was jolted by the blaring of its horn.

"Are you planning to drag your tail all the way home or do you want a ride?" a cheerful voice called to her after the horn had gotten her attention. Anne smiled involuntarily as she recognized Bill Rodgers' broad freckled face; and gratefully, if somewhat ungracefully, she stepped up on the high running board and joined him on the seat of his rusted, old truck for a short, bumpy ride back to her house.

# CHAPTER 9

"I brought you a present," Bill said, indicating a paper-backed booklet on the dashboard. The booklet was emblazoned with a broad border composed of various traffic signs; and even as she was being jostled about, Anne was able to read the two words on the cover, printed in large letters above the state logo. *Driving Manual,* it said.

"If you're going to be living here in Fairfield you'd better be serious about learning to drive. There just aren't any jobs here in town," Bill said; and he added, "You won't get far on that old bike." He gestured with his thumb toward the bed of his pickup.

Following his gesture, Anne looked through the rear window into the cargo portion of the truck and saw her bicycle, dusted off and equipped with new tires.

"Oh, Bill, thank you!" she said gleefully. "I can hardly wait to try it. I haven't been on a bicycle in almost ten years."

"You can try it out right now if you like," Bill replied as he parked the truck alongside the carriage house. Anne joined him at the rear of the truck and helped him unload the bike; and finding herself unable to resist the temptation to ride, she was soon wheeling it around the crescent driveway. At first she wobbled a little, but found herself gaining confidence with each turn of the pedals.

"This is terrific!" she called to Bill as she started around the drive for a second time.

"You're not too hard to please," he called back with a grin.

The next time around Anne pulled the bike up alongside the carriage house and stood it carefully alongside the building by its kickstand.

Bill handed her the net bag with one hand and the driving manual with the other. "By the way," he said. "They asked me at the license branch about the nature of your visa. In fact, they almost went into a tailspin. Nobody from a foreign country ever wanted to get a license in Fairfield before."

"Actually," Anne told him. "I don't need a visitor's visa. My mother was from the United States, and I was born here. While my father was alive I never thought about living here, but after his death Aunt Aggie wanted me to come; and since my mother was raised in this country..." She shrugged and said quietly, "I thought I might belong here."

The way she said the words "belong here," led Bill Rodgers to wonder if the lovely creature before him had ever really belonged anywhere. His heart was touched, but he merely said gruffly, "Well, good, you won't have any problems about your license then." As he walked away, he added, "Study the manual until you know it backwards and forwards and then you can take the test for your permit. After that, I'll teach you to drive."

The last part was said in such a matter-of-fact matter that Anne giggled involuntarily. "I just hope I'm easy to teach," she said.

The next few days were busy ones for Anne. Every day there was housecleaning to be done, and she gradually began to familiarize herself with the contents of the various closets and chests in the house. Because it would have been silly to keep things she couldn't use, she also began to sort through Aunt Aggie's personal effects.

On Saturday morning she rode her bike to town to purchase some toiletries. At a number of homes, she saw yard sales in progress. In England, local churches sometimes held jumble sales and there were second-hand stores that bought old clothes and household goods for resale; but Anne had not known that in the United States people would openly sell items they no longer needed from tables set up on their front lawns. Apparently there was no shame to it and everybody seemed to be having a good time, both buyers and sellers.

At one house Anne stopped to browse and enjoyed a pleasant conversation with a harried young mother who had several children running wildly about her. While looking at the items on sale, it occurred to Anne that a yard sale would be a perfect way to dispose of those things of Aunt Aggie's that she would never use. As she wanted to have her sale before she found a job that would take all of her time, she knew she needed to begin preparations at once.

On Sunday she dressed once more in her conservative navy skirt and white blouse and walked to the church she had attended with her aunt during her earlier visits. After the services, she was almost overwhelmed with welcome from people who remembered her as a teenager, people who remembered Aunt Agatha telling all about her, and people who had simply loved her aunt and were happy to meet one of Agatha's relatives. She received half a dozen invitations to Sunday dinner and found it difficult to decline, so firmly were the offers pressed.

Although Anne turned down all the dinner invitations, she did agree to take a drive with Mr. and Mrs. Bello later that afternoon, for that kind-hearted couple offered to take her to the cemetery to see where her aunt had been buried. After lunching alone in the sun room on sandwiches made of tinned chicken, she changed into her gray slacks for the afternoon outing with the Bellos.

The cemetery was far out on the edge of town and had little of the somber dreariness Anne had anticipated, being of the modern type where all of the memorial stones were flat ones set into the ground. The stones were therefore non-intrusive and the view across the slightly rolling fields was primarily one of grass and trees. Off to one side, in the older part of the cemetery, more elaborate above-ground monuments were visible; but even there the aspect was more charming and pleasant than dismal.

American cemeteries, Anne decided, were places where memories were recalled rather than places to indulge oneself in grief. The idea fit her beliefs perfectly. She knew as she gazed at the small aluminum holder, containing the card that identified Agatha Brownfield's grave, that her aunt was not really here in this spot any more than she was now in her house. In fact, there was more of Aunt Aggie in the house than here in a grave where the re-sodding had already taken hold to the extent that it looked as if the grass had been growing here forever.

Anne knew that she would sometimes visit this grave out of respect for her aunt's memory but that she would not come here to grieve. Wherever the spirit of Aunt Aggie had gone, it was not here.

The next grave belonged to Uncle Lester. Anne paused there also for a moment's prayer, for she had not been able to come to the States for his funeral either. She noted that his stone was a very simple one of deep blue marble with simple deep cut lettering, free of unnecessary curlicues.

As she and the Bellos strolled back toward the cemetery lane where the car was parked, she looked carefully at a number of grave markers to see what might be suitable for Aunt Aggie's grave. Pink marble, she decided, made exactly like Uncle Lester's and with Aunt Aggie's name and the dates of her birth and death carved in the same simple, clean lettering as had been used on her husband's stone. Anne decided she would make sure that the stone was of the exact same cut and size as Uncle Les's, a twin to his in every way except the color.

Satisfied with her decision regarding the stone, on the way back to town she asked Mr. Bello if he could locate a stonecutter who would do the work. Mr. Bello promised to look into the matter and get back to her when he had found someone reliable.

Mr. and Mrs. Bello then firmly changed the subject to one more pleasant; and before returning Anne to her home, the two insisted on taking her to an ice cream stand along the highway which had outside tables covered with brightly striped umbrellas. Mrs. Bello insisted Anne have the ice cream topped strawberry shortcake, which was the specialty of the restaurant, and Anne enjoyed the dessert tremendously.

Afterward, when the old couple returned Anne to her home, Mrs. Bello leaned out the car window and patted Anne's hand before allowing her to enter the house.

"You're a good girl, Anne," she said. "I'm glad you're here to live in Aggie's house. It's right that you should be here. The mister and I heard there's someone wantin' to buy it, but you just hang on. Aggie would want you to."

Anne promised to keep the house if there was any way possible to do so and told the two good-bye, promising to visit when she could.

After having attended church that Sunday, Anne was a stranger in the community no more. Every day the phone rang several times as people pursued her friendship and did their best to make sure she wasn't lonely.

In between answering the phone and cleaning and inspecting every item in the large house, Anne spent hours studying the driver's manual and writing letters to Janet. She even wrote a short note to the two Mr. Garolds, her former bosses, to fulfill a promise to let them know "how she got on".

At mid-morning each day she checked the mailbox, which Bill had fastened to the house near her front door, always hoping for a letter from Janet; but although a return note was eventually to be received from the younger of the two Mr. Garolds, she received no news from her friend. Even though she knew quite well that Janet was not much of a letter writer, she was none-the-less hurt that Janet had apparently forgotten her entirely once she was out of sight. It seemed she must make a home in this new country if ever she was to have a home at all, for there was even less for her in England than she had supposed.

In the evenings, too tired for other activities, Anne watched the telly in the little sitting room just off the hall, near the kitchen. Although she encountered many programs which were familiar to her, there were a wealth of shows she had never seen before, some not so good, others very good, but none good enough to keep her awake much past dusk. Yet, tired as she was from her busy days, every evening Anne reminded herself that she must get her license and she must get a job. Although she felt she could be happy in her new home, she knew in her heart that her decision to keep the house was unrealistic. She knew she could not afford it, but she *couldn't bear not to keep it.* Someday she might *have* to part with it but she meant to make every effort to stave off that day for as long as possible; particularly since, as time went by, she began to have more and more associations within her adopted community.

# CHAPTER 10

Anne had been in Fairfield for only a little over a week the day Rick, the boy from the hardware store, rang her doorbell. "Your grass is getting high," he said. "Do you have a lawn mower?"

"I'm not sure," Anne answered, "But Bill Rodgers is working in the carriage house. I'm sure he'll know."

"Well," Bill said when asked, "I think there is one here somewhere, but it hasn't been used for a while. Aggie had a gardener do the heavy work the last couple of years." Then he added helpfully, "I think I can locate it, though, and I'm pretty sure I can get it in shape to use."

As he spoke, Bill wiped his hands off on an old rag and then extended one hand to the young man, "How are you, Rick?" he asked jovially.

"Just fine, sir,"

"Did you come to help Anne with the lawn?"

"I sure did."

"Well, Anne, isn't the gardener still coming?" Bill asked

"If he is, he'll just have to stop," Anne said firmly, "I can't afford a gardener."

"Well then, I guess Rick and I will have to get the lawn mower going. You go on inside and we'll work on it."

"I need to know how to run it myself," Anne said. "I can't depend on you two all the time."

"When we get the lawn mower going we'll call you and teach you how to use it," Bill said, while he suppressed a grin at the thought of the cool young woman before him pushing the crotchety old mower around the large yard.

A couple of hours later, the two called Anne outside. The lawn mower was making a painfully loud roar, so apparently it now worked. Several times, the men shut it off so Anne could learn to start it up. Bill also instructed her about adding fuel and how to use the mower safely, but he seemed worried as he watched her strain at the pull cord to start up the machine.

"I'd like to mow the lawn for you, but I can't today. I have an appointment with my advisor at the university, and Rick has to go to work this afternoon. I'll do it for you tomorrow, if you like."

"No," Anne said, "I think I should learn to do it myself."

"Well," Bill said, "I like an independent woman, don't you Rick?" He gave the boy a playful punch in the shoulder and offered him a ride home. Then the two roared off in Bill's truck and Anne was left alone with the lawn mower.

It started beautifully and Anne had mowed several not-so-straight swaths across the back of the lawn when a pebble hidden in the tall grass was thrown by the lawn mower against her bare leg. Startled by the sudden pain, she allowed the motor to throttle down too much and it died.

After she recovered her composure she began to pull the lawn mower's starter cord. She pulled...and pulled...and pulled. The lawn mower made only an anemic wheeze. It refused to start. Determined not to let it get the best of her, she pulled the cord again...and again—until she was roughly shoved aside.

"What do you think you're doing?" Matt Stevens demanded, gripping her tightly by her upper arms.

"Don't you know there's a gardener for this kind of thing?"

"There may be," said Anne irritably, "But I can't afford a gardener."

"It's none of your concern while this house is still a part of an estate of which I am executor," Matt told her.

"You may be the executor, but I believe I am the heiress," Anne told him icily. "If you want to throw your money around, that's fine; but I believe I am entitled to whatever money remains in the estate when probate ends, and I'd appreciate it if you would not waste MY money on gardeners."

The glare in Matt's narrowed eyes caused little green glints to appear in their sky-blue irises. He looked at Anne for a long moment without saying a word; then he turned and gave the starter cord of the lawn mower a savage pull. The lawn mower roared to life and Matt began to push it. He walked in a long, perfectly straight line from the rear corner of the lot, where Anne remained standing, to the front edge half a block away. Then he turned and started back again in an equally straight line parallel to the first. The steady way he gripped the mower and the powerful long strides he took brooked no interference.

Anne glared at him while he mowed three full rows. Then she walked to the back porch and seated herself on the porch swing with arms crossed tightly across her chest as if to restrain the anger that threatened to erupt; but in spite of her restrained anger, her eyes remained on Matt.

He was an impressive sight to watch, even dressed as he was in sweat pants and a tee shirt. Apparently he had been jogging when he happened upon Anne and her lawn mower. His gray sweat pants must have been wet with sweat, for although they were ordinary, baggy-type sweat pants they were clinging to the length of his extravagantly long, lean legs. The tee shirt was of the sleeveless type. Surprisingly Matthew, an attorney, had muscles which surpassed those of Bill Rodgers who had been doing carpentry all summer.

"He must know how good looking he is," Anne thought viciously; "but good looking or not, attorney or not, he needn't think he can tell me what to do!"

The mower hummed steadily on for more than an hour. Seated on the porch in a flood of bright sunlight, Anne felt herself becoming uncomfortably warm. Gradually her anger over Matt Stevens' highhandedness began to diminish. It really was hot outside. Mowing the lawn must be torture under the hot sun.

Finally, Anne's inborn courtesy vanquished the last of her anger and she went into the house to prepare some lemonade; but first she stepped, with slight shame at this evidence of her vanity, into the small powder room, which had been built in what was formerly a butler's pantry, in order to check her appearance. She was appalled at the sight of her dust and sweat-streaked face in the mirror. There was no time for fresh make-up, but she washed off the dirt and brushed quickly through her hair before returning to the kitchen to prepare the lemonade.

When the lemonade was finished, she dumped a full tray of ice cubes into the pitcher and carried the frosty beverage out to the porch along with a couple of glasses. She planned to pour a glass for Matt and make him stop mowing to drink it. In *fact,* he had mowed enough for one day and he could just stop altogether and sit down and cool off, she thought; but as she stepped through the back door she heard the mower shut off and saw that Matt had ended his mowing near the carriage house and was now wheeling the mower in through the open garage door.

Anne hastily poured a glass of lemonade for Matt, but before she could take it to him he came striding across the back yard. Stopping in front of her, he took the glass from her hand and drank most of it down in one long swallow. He then handed the glass back to her; and as she took it, she suddenly found her arms gripped by his hands once again. This time, however, Matt was not yelling at her. His lips came down against hers. She felt them press demandingly, bruising her own unresisting mouth. She felt the coolness of the drink he had just swallowed and tasted the lemon of his breath along with the salt warmth of his sweat. She swayed against him and nearly fell over as he set her aside, having touched nothing except her lips and her arms...having touched her everywhere to the depths of her heart.

She watched him in confusion as he strode away. When he reached the street he turned toward her and said, almost angrily, "I'll pick you up at eight."

# CHAPTER 11

At first Anne did not move. As if transfixed by his kiss, she watched Matt turn the corner at the end of the block and stride off toward the north. Only then did she leave the porch to go back into the house, slamming the door behind her even though there was now no one to hear it slam. "That obnoxious man!" she said aloud, only to be startled at the sound of her own voice in the empty house. "What makes him think I'll be ready at eight o'clock just because he says so? I might have other plans."

But a little voice deep within her replied mockingly, "But you don't have other plans, do you, Dearie?" and without fully realizing it, Anne was already checking the clock to see how long remained until time for Matt to return. Time enough, she decided, to wash her hair, press her sage green blouse and have a soak in the tub.

The combination of repressed anger within and reflected sage from without caused her usually hazel eyes to glow very green as she answered her front doorbell that evening. Above the blouse her hair was a coppery cloud, which swept seductively across her forehead nearly covering one eye. In a characteristic gesture, she reached to tuck the offending hair behind one ear as she stepped aside to allow Matt to enter the house.

"Don't do that," he said, grasping her wrist before she could disturb her hair. "It looks nice that way."

"Well, I need to see where I'm going as well," she snapped tartly.

"Everyone else will certainly want to see where you're going," he complimented her. Stepping back a pace while still holding on to her wrist, he allowed his eyes to roam over her from her toes in their strappy, high-heeled sandals to the top of her head, approximately at the height of his shoulders. "You look beautiful." he added simply.

Anne cast her eyes downward. "Well, where are you taking me?" she asked briskly, in order to cover her embarrassment. She pulled her wrist loose and turned to get a small green handbag from the hall table near the door. "I hope we're going to eat. I'm starved."

"Don't worry," he answered. "I'll feed you." He held the door open and led her outside to the red sports car, which was gleaming brightly as if it too had been washed and spiffed up for this occasion.

Anne soon found herself roaring down the highway, the car exhibiting all the unleashed power she had suspected it might have. Perhaps Matt noticed that she was somewhat uncomfortable, hurtling down the road on what, to her sensibilities seemed to be the wrong side, for he soon slowed down to a more reasonable speed and began to flirt with her outrageously.

When the car finally pulled off the road at their destination, Anne felt brief consternation to see that they were stopping at a large hotel. Matt laughed delightedly at her expression. "On my honor," he said, "we are going to the public rooms only. There's a really fine restaurant here."

The restaurant was indeed fine. The dining area was one enormous room separated into a half dozen individual areas by the means of divider walls that extended two-thirds of the way from floor to ceiling and were topped with wide shelves on which antique brass and copper implements were displayed. The tables were covered with pastel colored cloths with matching napkins and candles, a different color for each dining area. By Matt's request, he and Anne were seated in an area where the linen was of palest green to compliment her outfit.

During the meal Anne said little, but derived considerable pleasure from listening to Matt's banter and watching his hands across the table as he handled his silver or drank wine from a crystal tumbler. She had almost forgotten the high-handed way in which he had arranged for their evening together until he asked her once more about selling the house.

"I told you I do not intend to sell the house," Anne answered. "I thought I made myself clear."

"I wondered if you might have changed your mind after thinking it over," he said gently. "You're in an entirely new life, in a new home and a new country. You know no one here, have no family, and," he added, "you're very young. You should be having fun. A house like that is a big responsibility."

"My responsibility," Anne told him. "Not yours, I think." After that conversation the shine was gone from the evening. Anne could no longer take Matt's attentions seriously, knowing as she did that they were motivated by his intent to convince her to sell the house. She wondered why he cared so much. Surely concern for her well-being must not be part of his ethical responsibility simply because he had been her aunt's attorney. There must be some other reason. She remembered that Matt had mentioned that the buyer in line for the house wanted her house and none other. Perhaps that was it; perhaps the buyer was another client, a client more important than she. She remembered that Bill Rodgers had suggested she ask Matt who the buyer was and found herself asking him.

Matt hesitated a moment before answering her question, as if carefully considering his answer. "I'm not at liberty to say, Anne. The buyer doesn't want to have his name divulged, but he is willing to pay you a very good price. You would not go wrong by accepting his offer."

"I would go wrong if I sold the house Aunt Aggie left me," Anne retorted shortly.

Matt reached across the table and patted her hand gently. "Don't get all stirred up. I don't want you to be angry at me about this. I'll tell you what. The buyer is represented by a local real estate agent. The agent is planning to come to see you and tender his offer. What say I just let him handle the matter from now on? I don't want it to come between us."

"There's nothing to handle." Anne said. "I'm not selling the house." She picked up her handbag and pushed back her chair.

Matt signaled the waiter and handed him a folded bill, shaking his head in response to the waiter's promise to return with his change. Taking Anne by the arm, he led her from the restaurant.

The route Matt drove on the return trip was long and circuitous because he wished to prolong the evening, but he could not recapture the light-hearted mood he and Anne had shared earlier. Anne believed that his attentions to her were simply to convince her to sell Aunt Aggie's house, and she refused to allow him any further satisfaction from his efforts.

When he turned into her driveway, Anne requested that he drive to the side door rather than stop at the front of the house. As soon as she was inside the door on the tiny landing between the basement stairs and those to the kitchen, she turned with the intention of saying goodnight to Matt and entering the house alone.

Matt, however, was not to be dissuaded from entering. "I'd prefer to come in for a few minutes, Anne," he said pleasantly. "I'm thirsty. I believe I'd like another glass of that lemonade, if you don't mind."

Although Matt could not see her blush in the dim light on the stairs, Anne turned swiftly away at the mention of lemonade, which invoked the memory of the kiss with which she would associate that beverage forever after.

Matt took advantage of the moment; and, with his hand on the small of her back, guided her up the few steps into the kitchen. He then made himself at home, pouring lemonade from the 'fridge and appropriating tea biscuits from the counter top.

"We left the restaurant without dessert," he commented as he seated himself on a counter stool and began to munch a cookie.

A few moments later, Anne stepped into the small sitting room where she usually watched the television in order to change to some comfortable slippers she was sure she had left there. Somehow Matt managed to join her with such speed that she almost bumped into him as she turned back around after kicking off the tiresome high-heeled sandals.

The last thing she saw was Matt's slender hand resting on the light switch as he pressed it downward. With the room plunged into darkness, she found herself enveloped in his strong arms, her face resting against the nubby texture of his shirt. When his lips came down on hers she tried at first to resist, but found herself instead drinking deeply of his kiss, drowning herself in his essence. The world ceased; for the moment there was only Matt, Matt's hands and his lips, the supple strength of his body pressed against hers.

There was a comfortable sofa in the room, one where Anne had already fallen asleep several nights while watching the telly. Now, somehow she was lying on the sofa with Matt kneeling beside her.

His lips never left hers as his fingers began to run through her hair. When he finally released her lips and laid his cheek against hers and began to whisper almost inaudible words of endearment into her ear, she offered no resistance and had no will to resist until she heard the sound of a clock striking in the hall, the magnificent grandfather clock that stood sentinel alongside the table near the front door. No other sound could have penetrated Anne's consciousness as thoroughly as the sound of the clock in the hall of Aunt Aggie's house.

Struggling almost frantically, she fought her way loose from Matt's arms; and taking advantage of his momentary confusion at her abrupt change of behavior, managed to escape his embrace and run from the room. By the light of the moon shining through the fanlight above the front door she ran up the staircase and shut herself in her room, closing the door behind her and snapping the lock. She threw herself across her bed as the clock ceased chiming.

A few moments later she heard Matt's car pull slowly from the drive as she lay there sobbing because the love she felt for him was only reciprocated by his need to convince her to sell her house. She had thought she would never know desire, had thought her heart would never have a home. Now that she knew love, she also knew the awful emptiness of love unrequited.

# CHAPTER 12

The first rose came as the clock struck 9:00 the following morning. The doorbell rang several times before Anne, dressed in the knee length tee shirt she had slept in, her eyes tear-swollen, peeked through the curtained windows flanking the massive front door. At first she saw only a striped shirt sleeve, but then its wearer turned and she saw the insignia "Blossom Place", across his shirt pocket. She opened the door far enough to accept the long slender box and carried it to the sun room where she opened it at the round oak table. The single white rose was flanked by green fern and tiny white baby's breath blossoms. Opening the small white envelope she read the laconic message, "Apologies, Matt."

She laid the card aside wearily, knowing no apology would ever be a substitute for the true caring she craved; but there was no use wasting the delicate beauty of the flower, so she arranged the contents of the box in a nearby vase which she left in the middle of the round table.

At 10:00, now dressed and somewhat recovered, Anne answered the doorbell again to receive another slender box. Two yellow roses, no card.

At 11:00 the broadly-grinning delivery boy brought three pink roses.

As noon neared, Anne caught herself watching for the small blue delivery van which had visited her three times already that day. She was not disappointed when the boy came with four deep red roses. There was still no further card. Anne added the additional blooms to the wide mouthed milk glass vase where she had placed the first rosebud and which was now overflowing with blooms.

At 1:00 the florist delivery van appeared for the final time, bearing two velvet-leafed, perfect white orchids. She opened the envelope with trembling hands, "A dozen apologies—please forgive me, Matt." She caught back a sob as she added the flowers to the bulging display on the round table. She had almost dared to hope he cared, but this was no message of affection; it was damage-control, she decided.

The man was truly sorry he had taken a wrong turn with her because that would not accomplish his purpose which Anne knew with dull misery was to convince her to sell her house. Sent to her for such a purpose, the flowers were a *fragrant* mockery of the romance she yearned for.

She was not unduly surprised when the phone rang at 2:00. "Am I forgiven?" the deep rich tones of Matt's voice inquired.

Anne trembled with the effort to remain cool and seem nonchalant as she answered him crisply. "There was really no need to go to such expense simply because you caught me a little off guard. I believe I truly was feeling a little homesick and vulnerable. It was really I who took advantage of you."

Anne heard the sharp intake of breath at the other end of the phone line even as her own face blanched as the words tumbled unbidden from her lips. Had she really said that? Well, it was far better to seem sophisticated and unconcerned than to fall helplessly at the man's feet. She heard herself add, "It won't happen again."

"That's my line," Matt replied dryly.

"Good, then we're fully agreed," Anne said, hearing in her voice a biting tone she had not known she was capable of creating.

"Let's just say we had a mutual misunderstanding," Matt said softly. "Apparently we got off on the wrong foot, but we still need to get along because we have business to transact. I'll need your signature on some papers soon. I'll contact you as soon as my secretary has them ready."

With that, he rang off, leaving Ann holding the uncaring phone receiver in her hand until it beeped a loud reminder to replace it in its cradle. Business again! She wondered how Matt had not noticed her heart, which in spite of her biting words had leaped across town along the phone wires toward the place of refuge for which it yearned. Apparently she would have no trouble deceiving him of her true feelings, which was one small blessing; for she knew she would die on the spot if Matt were to suspect the nature of her unrequited feelings for him.

Even when one's heart breaks, there is still work to be done. This was the case with Anne; so over the next days she thought of Matt as little as possible—still quite a great deal—as she worked furiously at the task she had set herself, to go through all the contents of the house and organize all the items she needed to dispose of at the yard sale she planned.

One week after her dinner date with Matt, the local paper contained her advertisement for the sale to be held the following Saturday morning. When she opened the tabloid-sized paper to check her listing, she found the front page bore unusually large headlines extending across the entire width of the printing area: *"Industry comes to Fairfield"*

She read with growing interest the account of the small manufacturer of novelty items who planned to re-locate his growing business from a small nearby city to a new building to be built in Fairfield's *"newly zoned industrial complex"* at the north edge of the town. There, she read, the business would have space to build a large, modern building with room for expansion as necessary.

A number of jobs would open for the hard-pressed working force of Fairfield. At first, there would be construction jobs; later machine operators and packers and shippers would be needed as well as support staff such as bookkeepers, clerks and secretaries. Only a core staff would be coming from the previous location. It was the intention of Novelties, Inc. to recruit their help from the town of Fairfield and its surrounding rural areas. Near the bottom of the page a small related story caught Anne's eye.

*"Residents protest industry,"* the headline announced. In this article, Anne read of a planned protest meeting organized by residents who lived near the proposed industrial complex. Matthew Stevens, Fairfield attorney, was to address the group at a meeting to take place two weeks hence at the gymnasium of the local high school. Anne read the article with some dismay. How could citizens of Fairfield protest incoming industry? Why the area cried out for jobs! Nearly everyone she had met since moving to town drove thirty, even forty miles to work. How could Matt be a party to such a senseless protest?

Sighing, she set aside the paper. Bill was due in a few minutes to discuss the final preparations for the yard sale. He would also be coming Saturday morning to help her bring all the merchandise upstairs from the basement where, during the last couple of weeks of intensive cleaning and sorting, she had stashed the numerous articles she had decided to sell.

Within half an hour of Bill's arrival, he and Anne had determined the arrangement of the sale. Sawhorses and lumber from the carriage house would form one long table. The picnic table and benches would be pressed into service to form more display surfaces and several card tables Anne had found could be used for merchandise—at least until they were sold. Viewing the clothing that was for sale, Bill promised to rig a temporary clothesline for the hangers. He would also carry out the heavy hall table. With its drop leaves extended it was quite large.

At barely 5:00 on Saturday morning Bill arrived to put their plans into effect. The previous day he had insisted on mowing the lawn for Anne to spare her the frustration of the recalcitrant lawn mower, and he had raked the grass clippings from the side yard so they would not collect on damp shoes in the early-morning dew.

The sale tables looked quite nice arranged on the freshly clipped lawn in a semi-circle that followed the path of the driveway. He and Anne worked quickly to transfer the massive collection of sale items from the floor of the basement to the sale area, but some items Bill would not permit Anne to sell.

"No, no, don't sell that," he said, rescuing a two-tier glass coffee pot from her arms. "It might not be worth anything, but it's an old one. Better to check on its worth than find out after you sell it. If it's not worth much, you can still sell it to a second-hand dealer for about what you'd get today.

"It seems you've got some really good stuff here. Far better than the average sale."

Anne followed his advice and placed a number of items he suggested she keep on a wide shelve along the basement wall. There were still, however, an enormous number of useful articles to sell.

The semi-circular arrangement of makeshift sales counters was stocked none too soon. Although Anne had advertised her sale for 8:30 in the morning, cars began pulling up to the curb at barely 8:00.

Some of the first arrivals were inveterate yard sale shoppers who viewed the merchandise with practiced eye, snatching up bargains for re-sale later as well as for their own use. Other shoppers were acquaintances from church or curious townspeople who wanted to meet Anne or looked forward to buying something that had belonged to Agatha Brownfield because she had been well- admired.

Anne was at first nervous about talking to so many strangers, but soon relaxed in the friendly, bantering atmosphere that developed. Bill made a few suggestions to let an item go at a cheaper price while there was a willing buyer or to stand firm on a price that was already quite fair when a would-be purchaser pressed too hard. Mainly, however, he busied himself helping customers load bulky purchases in their cars or re-arranging merchandise as the stock swiftly dwindled, leaving Anne to handle the actual sales.

Although she was rapidly learning about U.S. money, the decimal system being quite logical to follow, Anne was at a loss making change with any speed. With a number of small jokes at her own ineptitude she allowed each customer to coach her through his or her own transaction.

At around 9:30, a renewed surge of shoppers had Anne fully occupied when she suddenly found herself looking up into the bluest eyes she had ever seen, eyes she would know anywhere.

"Karen and I thought we'd come see how your sale is going," he said, glancing around to see the items that remained.

Only then did Anne notice the small girl at her father's side. "Hello, Miss Long," Karen chirped cheerfully.

"Call me Anne, Honey," she said, dropping to the child's level to smile into the miniature blue eyes, so like Matt's "Your father does," she added pointedly, in order to remind that deceitful male that the non-business aspects of their relationship were entirely of his doing.

She then took Karen by the hand. Leaving Bill with the change box to take care of customers, she walked the child from table to table showing her odd knickknacks and furniture and weaving small tales about them as she went. The child's company was so welcome to her that she almost forgot the father as she visited with the delightful, pixie-like charmer.

Left alone, however, Matt soon tired of looking at the items for sale and came to reclaim his child. By then Karen had taken a fancy to a small pink unicorn planter which Anne would have given her willingly, but the child produced a shiny quarter from the pocket of her diminutive blue jeans and offered it gravely. With equal gravity Anne accepted the payment.

"I believe your father knows a really good florist," she told Karen as she wrapped the china piece in newspaper and put it into a bag. "Maybe he'll get you a green plant for this. A green plant is really much better than cut flowers, you know. Plants last; cut flowers soon die."

If Matt felt any sting from her words, he did not let on. Instead Anne heard him politely asking a favor. "There's a movie Karen is dying to see, Anne. It's not a kiddy picture exactly though it will only be a shade less boring, I'm afraid. It's more a family type film. I'd really appreciate it if you would come with us tomorrow afternoon. It's hard to take a little girl by myself. You know how it is, she sometimes needs to go to the ladies' room and I can't just ask a stranger to take her."

Of course the child needs a woman for company, Anne thought, as her heart responded to the memory of a dozen years without her own mother to attend her; but a second more analytical thought followed: Why didn't he ask Stella to join him and Karen?

Aloud she said to him, "I'm sure you'll find someone else to help you out. I'm quite busy." *You are not,* her treacherous heart shouted impatiently, *Go with them! Go with them!*

"Please come with us, Miss Long," Karen begged.

"I thought I told you to call me Anne," she heard herself saying and soon promised the child she would go with them to a matinee performance the following afternoon.

After the two had left, she waited on a couple of more customers before catching Bill with a quizzical look on his face.

"Old Matt is pretty slick, isn't he?" he commented. "He generally gets what he wants."

"It's not for him that I'm going," Anne insisted, turning her face toward Bill and exposing a naked, soft glow. "It's because of Karen."

Bill cleared his throat loudly but said nothing more, Anne wondered for a brief moment if he suspected her feelings for Matt; and if so, if he cared. Probably not, she decided.

From a practical standpoint she and Bill would have made a perfect couple. They would even look good together as each had coppery auburn hair, though his with freckles and hers with a creamy white complexion. They also shared a bond in having each cared deeply for Aunt Aggie; and Bill loved the old house as much as Anne did.

It was a shame that it was not Bill she had fallen for, but it was no use trying to change the way things were. Almost immediately she and Bill had fallen into a warm camaraderie, but there was no romance to it. It was almost as if Bill were the brother she had never had. They were close, very close; but Anne knew he was no more in love with her than she with him, though she had to admit that providence had been extremely wasteful in placing two such compatible creatures in close proximity and then arranging only friendship where romance would have been convenient. She sighed, knowing that love could not be forced. If it didn't just happen, it was not meant to be.

Even as she mused about the vagaries of human feelings, Anne continued to mechanically make small talk and deal with the problem of making change in U.S. money. More than a few customers smiled at the beautiful girl with her enchanting accent and said, "Just keep the change;" but Anne always insisted that they accept what was due to be returned. "I have to learn this sometime," she joked.

An hour later, during a lull in customers, Anne realized the sun was growing uncomfortably warm. She asked Bill if he wanted a drink, then entered the house to get glasses of ice water for him and her. The phone was ringing as she opened the door with an insistent sound which seemed to say it had been ringing for a long while. Anne's sale was forgotten when she heard the longed-for cadence of Janet Conard's voice at the other end of the line.

"Where have you been?" her friend demanded.

"Janet, is that you!" Anne exclaimed. "Why haven't you written or called?"

"I'll tell you all about it later. Right now, please come get me. I'm at the airport in some little city they tell me is fifty miles from Fairfield, and there's no public transportation!"

Anne thought quickly. Bill would have to go, if he would. Surely he would. His plans were to help with the yard sale all day, so there was nothing to conflict with him leaving. She could handle the rest of the sale herself.

"I'll send someone," Anne said. "A really nice man. Oh, Janet, I can hardly wait to see you! Just stay put. Bill will be there right away."

"Aren't you coming too?" Janet asked. "How will I know him?"

"I can't come right now. I'm having a yard sale."

"What's a yard sale?"

"Never mind," Anne told her. "Let me hang up now so I can send Bill after you. Don't worry, he'll know you. I'll give him your picture. Janet, I've missed you so much."

Tears of joy were wet in her eyes when she went outside to ask Bill to go for her friend.

# CHAPTER 13

"I told her I'd give you a picture, Bill; but you won't need one. She has striking black hair; it's curly and always sort of tousled. She's just a little taller than I, and her luggage is red plaid. She'll probably be wearing something red too. It's her favorite color."

"Don't worry; if I don't see a lady in red, I'll just holler, 'Hey Janet!'" Bill joked. "Now simmer down. You take care of the yard sale, and I'll go get your friend. It's a shame she's showed up unexpectedly, though," he teased. "I can tell how much you hate the idea of having company." He hung his arm about Anne's shoulder in mock commiseration.

"I knew you'd be nice the first time I asked you a favor," Anne said sweetly. Bill snorted at her retort and gave her a playful punch in the shoulder before climbing into his truck to go after Janet.

"Your friend is lucky she has a real gentleman to pick her up at the airport," he called out of the window as he drove away.

"Especially in that gorgeous truck," Anne shot back. For the next hour or so Anne continued to wait on customers, but in ever dwindling numbers. Gradually she was able to consolidate the remaining merchandise until all she had left was concentrated on the hall table and on one card table which had not yet been sold. She dragged the sawhorses and boards back to the carriage house; and after waiting on another straggling shopper, dragged the picnic table and benches, one at a time, back to the back yard Finally, there was little more that she could do, short of closing up shop.

She took the metal canister which had served as a cash box into the kitchen and spent a few minutes in the powder room freshening up for her friend's arrival, then returned to the site of the yard sale and sold the card table and an old magazine rack to a young couple who had arrived while she was inside. A half hour later, after fifteen minutes with no customers whatever, she was engaged in a transaction with an elderly woman who was buying several paperback books when Bill's truck came into view. Hastily, she made the woman a present of the books, before running toward the truck.

After some delighted hugging and squealing, the two young women were both talking at once when Bill put his arms around both waists and led them across the yard toward the picnic table.

"Janet and I picked up chicken for lunch," he said, indicating a carton already standing on the picnic table, which he must have put there while Janet and Anne were so occupied with their greetings that they were paying him no attention. "Let's eat out here and we can keep an eye out for any stray customers at the same time."

Bill left the two girls, still talking a mile a minute while he went into Anne's kitchen to get beverages. He returned shortly after with the drinks and some paper plates and napkins. He then insisted that the two young women visit and talk while he took care of the last few customers who dropped in. By now there was little left to sell except some items of Aggie's clothing. By flirting extravagantly with two elderly women who had come to the sale together, Bill managed to sell most of what remained, though at greatly reduced prices.

Meanwhile, Anne was finding out from Janet what turn of circumstances brought her to the United States.

"I thought you wouldn't ever leave Jeffrey," she mentioned.

"That's just the thing," Janet replied. "Jeffrey more or less left me, and there I was without a job."

"You lost your job, too!"

"I lost both at once," Janet mourned. "One day I went to work and the whole place was buzzing with news that the office

73

was being relocated somewhere to the north, away from the city. Some of the employees were being relocated; others were being given severance pay. Jeffrey was relocated. I was paid off. He left without even saying good-bye."

"Maybe he thought you'd be coming, too," Anne said.

"Hardly. Word went round that Jeffrey personally chose the girls who would be transferred. There was a lot of talk because a little blond thing who came to work there only a couple of months ago got the nod. She went; I didn't. Que sera."

"Oh, Janet. I'm so sorry"

"Don't give it a thought," Janet told her. "I'm not. It was obvious that Jeffrey never cared that much for me anyway. I just kept hanging on to a dream. It's probably a good thing it's ended. Now I can get on with my life."

Anne hugged her friend. "I'm so glad you're here."

"So am I," Janet replied; and Anne saw her look across the lawn to where Bill was unfastening the makeshift clothesline he had strung between the house and a carriage lamp pole. "I think I'm going to like it here; and anyway," she continued. "I had to come right away. Every letter you sent mentioned that lawyer trying to get you to sell your house. I thought I'd better get over here and see the sights before you turned up back in London."

"I hope it won't come to that," Anne said.

"Speaking of seeing the sights," Bill said as he rejoined them, "I want to volunteer myself as a guide. Ever since Anne arrived here, she's been so busy she's barely left the house. I thought there'd be plenty of time to take her places, but since your time is limited here, Janet, I think sightseeing should be a priority. I propose that tomorrow I take you both out for the day. It's supposed to be cooler tomorrow so I thought the amusement park might be..."

Bill was still speaking but Anne was no longer listening. Didn't Bill remember that she had agreed to go to a movie with

Karen and Matt tomorrow? Maybe she should beg off the movie. After all, she did have an unexpected out-of-town guest to consider. Janet would probably be very bored staying home all day.

Anne looked toward Janet, who was still hanging on every word Bill said, and back toward Bill, who seemed to be enjoying himself immensely. Maybe Bill hadn't forgotten about her date after all.

"Oh dear," Anne said quickly. "I can't go tomorrow. I have a prior engagement; but I hate for Janet to miss out on my account. Why don't you two go without me?"

"That's a shame," Janet said. "Bill, maybe we should wait until Anne can go."

"Oh, no," Anne said, "I don't want to spoil your fun."

"Please, don't say no," Bill pleaded; and Janet agreed to go with him the following day. They were to leave early in the morning.

After cleaning up the remains of the picnic, the two girls helped Bill return the drop leaf table to its place in the hall. Then he joined them at the round oak table in the sun room where they broke open the canister to tally up the receipts from the yard sale. There was a surprising amount of money in the can.

"You did great!" Bill said. "You could live for a month on this,"

"I could, perhaps; but I have other plans for this money," Anne said. "I want to order Aunt Aggie's grave marker. This money will go a long way toward paying for it. I intend to see Mr. Bello as soon as possible to see if he has located a stonecutter for me yet."

Janet instantly reached out her hand to give Anne a sympathetic pat as Bill applauded her decision in his usual offhand manner, "The exact right thing to do," he said.

Shortly afterward, Bill unloaded Janet's luggage from the truck and took his leave, mentioning that he was sure both girls were tired and he wanted Janet to get plenty of rest as he would be picking her up early the next morning.

He had hardly shut the door when Janet pounced on Anne, "Tell me you're not interested in Bill."

"I'm not interested in Bill," Anne replied, deadpan.

"How can you not be!" Janet exclaimed.

"It's quite simple," Anne told her. "I like him too much to find him romantically interesting. He felt like a great old friend the instant I met him,"

"The coast is clear then."

"Yes," Anne replied, enjoying her friend's pleasure. "The coast is clear."

"Tell me about the attorney," Janet said shrewdly, slightly narrowing her eyes as she spoke. "Did I read something between the lines of your letters?"

"Oh, no," Anne laughed. "There's nothing between us. I'm just a client, that's all." But Anne's laugh sounded a little forced to Janet and she was not convinced.

"What kind of man is he?" she questioned; and then as she pumped gently, Anne began to tell her all about Matt Stevens and Janet could not mistake the softening of her jaw and the sparkle in her eye as she spoke of him and of Karen, his daughter.

You've lost so much, my friend; she thought. I hope this time you'll be a winner. Beneath the folded pleats of her bright red skirt, Janet superstitiously crossed her fingers.

# CHAPTER 14

Janet had never been easy to waken; so after traveling for hours, arriving in the United States and being instantly caught up in the flow of Anne's life, followed by talking most of the night, she was nearly impossible to rouse on Sunday morning. At first Anne called her gently; then she shook her. Eventually she crossed the hall to the bathroom and returned to the guest room with a tumbler of water. After liberally sprinkling Janet's tip-tilted nose and the translucent lids of her eyes, Anne was eventually rewarded with the beginnings of a stir.

"Wake up now or I'll pour the whole glass on you," she threatened.

"Let me sleep," Janet begged.

"Bill will be here in fifteen minutes," Anne warned.

"I'm getting up; I'm getting up," Janet grumbled; as she slowly stretched herself upright and swung her slender legs over the edge of the bed. "I'm still so tired though, I'm going to look a fright."

"No, you won't," Anne answered. "You never do."

And, in fact, when Janet was through showering and had dressed in slim white slacks and a red pull-over trimmed with white stitching, she looked sensational, which Bill, who had arrived nearly a half hour before she finally skipped down the circular staircase, was quick to remark upon.

With cool unconcern, Janet merely patted him on the shoulder as she walked by on the way to the kitchen. "I'll just have a cup of tea and some toast before we go," she told Bill, giving him a flirtatious backward glance as she passed him. "Will you join me?"

Bill glanced at his watch with some dismay, but followed her obediently to the kitchen where he toasted bread for them both and liberally spread it with jam. Before the two had finished breakfasting and set out for their trip, Anne had been treated to the sight of Bill Rodgers literally eating from Janet Conard's hand.

"He acts besotted," she thought.

It was easy to see in what direction the two were heading, apparently with no resistance or dragging of feet on either part. Those two are so uncomplicated, Anne thought; and forgetting Janet's recent disappointment with Jeffrey, whom her friend had longed for and dreamed of for several years, and forgetting also that Janet might soon have to return home, leaving Bill behind, Anne envied the dark headed girl for being so lucky.

As Matt and Karen were not to come for Anne until early afternoon, there was no reason for her to miss church; but by the time she had cleaned up the kitchen mess created by her untidy guests it was growing late. She hurried upstairs and dressed quickly in a shawl-collared blouse of palest yellow with a not-too-short, but sassy skirt of charcoal gray, and conservative high-heeled pumps of gun metal patent. The blush she brushed across her delicate cheek bones contained a hint of brown to compliment the yellow of her blouse. She also stroked some green and some brown-tone eye shadow across her lids, blending the two colors skillfully, until they emphasized her hazel eyes without being obvious. When she picked up her small handbag to leave the house, she looked as stunning in her conservative apparel as Janet had looked in her stylish, coordinated outfit.

The opening organ selection was already being played when Anne slipped quietly through the double doors of the Methodist Church of Fairfield. Seated near the back, she saw Mr. and Mrs. Bello; and that kind couple immediately moved over to allow Anne to slip in beside them. As Anne took her seat, Mrs. Bello reached over and gave Anne's hand an affectionate pat, her round face wreathed in a welcoming smile.

Anne, who had been without her mother's love for years and had known the compensation of her aunt's affection during only brief periods of her life, felt as loved and welcome as she had ever felt. She felt herself relax as she settled into the pew to listen to the proceedings. There was a friendly, homespun tone to the small town church services that she had never experienced before and which she found very comforting.

She enjoyed the sensation of simply being there so much that her concentration began to drift.

Across the aisle, a woman was feeding a baby with a small yellow nursery bottle. Anne found herself engrossed in the sight of the infant, who was sucking greedily at his plastic nipple. Imagining what it must be like to be the mother of such a little charmer, Anne realized that there was nothing she would like more; but she had little reason to hope that life, which had given her little of lasting relationships in the past, would see fit to provide her with a husband and child anytime in the foreseeable future.

In fact, she thought wryly, the only man I have ever cared for is not interested in me—he wants my house. She fully believed that she would never see Matt Stevens again if she once entered into an agreement for the sale. The prospect of losing contact with Matt was only a shade less devastating to contemplate than the loss of the house.

After a while, Anne heard shuffling sounds as the church congregation stood to sing a hymn. She guiltily withdrew her attention from the pleasing sight of the baby's chubby hands and eager little mouth, and from the chain of thought they engendered. Hastily, she turned the pages of her hymnal to page 248 in order to join the singing.

Following the services, Anne once more basked in the warmth of the greetings of Aggie's old friends, and in the cheerful welcome of churchgoers nearer her own age, young people she knew would soon be her own friends. Along with the Bellos, she joined the throng slowly threading its way out the double doors where the minister shook hands with each person before allowing him or her to leave the sanctuary.

"Glad to see you again, Miss Long," he said pleasantly, as he gave her hand a quick, firm grasp before reaching out for the hand of the next in line.

"Mrs. Bello, did I hear your granddaughter is coming soon?" Anne heard him ask.

"She is for sure," Mrs. Bello replied. "I've asked your daughter to come keep her company one day next week. Do you think she can make it?"

"You just let my wife know; I'm sure it can be worked out," he told her, then passed her on out the door as he continued in a practiced manner cheerfully greeting each member of his congregation with a personal word or two.

Outside, Anne looked around for Mr. Bello who had left the church ahead of the women while they were still engaged in conversation. She found him when he placed a hand on her shoulder.

"There you are girl," he said. "I've been looking for you. I've got a fella wants to come over to see you about that monument for Aggie's grave. Would it be okay if he comes sometime tomorrow?"

Anne grinned at the friendly man with the booming voice. "I was just looking for you to see if you'd found someone for me. I'll stay home tomorrow until he shows up. I won't feel right until I have the stone ordered."

"Mrs. Bello has some news she'll be wantin' to tell you. Our granddaughter's coming today to stay with us for a while."

"So I heard," Anne said.

"Come to dinner with us today, Anne," Mrs. Bello said as she joined the two. "You can stay and meet our son and his wife. They're only going to be here a couple of days this time, but we're going to be seeing a lot more of them in the future." She beamed as she continued. "For a while they're going to be doing a lot of running back and forth, but they hope to move here permanently within a few months. They're going to let Vickie Anne stay with us until they get settled!"

"Mama is so excited!" Mr. Bello said.

"I can't make it today," Anne told them with a smile at their obvious joy. "I promised Matthew Stevens I'd go with him to a movie this afternoon to help with Karen."

"Well, have a good time!" Mrs. Bello exclaimed. "Matt's a fine boy. Your aunt thought a lot of him," she added with a firm nod of her head.

Anne knew that Mrs. Bello had just put her seal of approval on a relationship between her and Matt which did not exist, but she did not try to disavow Mrs. Bello of her hastily drawn conclusion. Instead she turned the conversation to a certain distraction by asking, "How old is your granddaughter?"

Before Mrs. Bello had tired of the subject of her granddaughter, nearly all the other churchgoers had gone.

"Come along, Mama," Mr. Bello urged several times.

Finally Anne accepted a ride for the few scant blocks to her home in order to assist Mr. Bello in his efforts to persuade his wife to leave the churchyard.

Once at home, Anne made a meal of buttered bread and cold fried chicken left over from Bill's purchase of the previous day. She opened a can of Aunt Aggie's tinned peaches for her dessert. "I've hardly had a hot meal since I came to the States," she thought as she sat down to the unappealing lunch.

She had consumed very little of the meal when she cleared the remains from the table and went upstairs to freshen up.

# CHAPTER 15

Almost exactly on the hour appointed by Matt Stevens to pick Anne up for the movie, Anne heard her front door bell ring. When she lifted the curtain, she saw no one through the glass panel; but when she opened the door she saw that it was Karen who had rung the bell. The child was so small that she did not reach as high as the glass part of the door. Anne could see Matt standing in the driveway, half-hidden by the corner of the house, imparting confidence to the little girl.

Karen's upturned eyes gazed solemnly at Anne, "Are you ready to go Miss Long?" she asked. "My daddy said I could come to the door for you all by myself."

"I am ready," Anne told her. "Just let me get my handbag." She retreated into the house but came back very quickly so she would not keep the child waiting.

As Anne stepped outside, Karen reached up her hand and said ingenuously, "Daddy says we must be very nice to you, because you are being very kind to go to the movie with us."

Anne felt crushed because she was reminded that the outing with Matt and his small daughter, to which she had been looking forward with pleasure, was simply a matter of convenience to him—a favor from one friend to another which he would accept with polite gratitude but which had little meaning beyond the moment. It hurt to be reminded of his lack of personal interest in her presence.

As Karen and Anne approached the car, Matt held the door wide open and smiled broadly. In spite of herself, Anne then began to forget the pain engendered by her renewed realization of her lack of importance to Matt. His manners were impeccable even if they did mask an indifferent heart and he was most certainly a handsome escort. Of course, she was rapidly growing to love Karen, so perhaps she would have a good time going out with the two of them after all.

Matt helped Karen into the back seat and closed the door only after being sure that Karen had fastened her seat belt and that Anne's skirt was wholly within the car. He then went around the front of the car to the driver's seat with a kind of jaunty lope to his walk.

His first words to Anne were, "I thought we might have two English nannies for Karen today. I hear you have a house guest."

Anne forgot to be irritated at being called a nanny in her surprise that he had already heard about Janet's visit.

"Yes, I do," she said. "A very good friend was kind enough to take her sightseeing today, seeing as I had a prior engagement." Having said this, Anne wished she had said the words in a slightly more pleasant tone. Her voice had given no clue of the pleasure she felt in the company of this man and his child.

"News certainly travels fast around here," she commented.

"Yes, indeed it does," Matthew said. "As a matter of fact," he said gravely. "The Town Council met in emergency session not one hour after your friend arrived."

Anne looked at him quizzically.

With mock seriousness, he continued, "They met to discuss the pending economic crisis. The street department put in an emergency request for additional funds to maintain the road passing in front of your house. Every man in town under the age of forty is expected to drive past your house at least a half dozen times a day during the next month. The superintendent of streets says that the South River Road absolutely cannot handle the increased traffic without additional funds for emergency repair."

"Why he's pulling my leg," Anne thought.

Matt continued, "And a resolution has been passed that you are required by law to give at least twenty-four hour's notice of the arrival of any additional beautiful, young English women."

83

Anne shook her head at Matt's sly teasing, but soon found that, particularly in the presence of his small daughter, he could be a quite entertaining companion. During the half hour drive to the small nearby city where they would attend the movie matinee, he teased both Karen and Anne unmercifully.

The theater was located in a large shopping mall, and Anne was entranced as soon as they entered. There were half a dozen different theaters in operation at one time, sharing a common lobby. The pictures showing in the various theaters had all been widely advertised in commercials which appeared on television shows Anne had watched since arriving in the States. The feature Matt and Karen had chosen to attend was one Anne had hoped to see.

Prior to entering the theater where their movie was to be shown, Anne took Karen to the ladies' loo. Afterward she stood in line with Matt to buy a huge bucket of popcorn as well as drinks for each of the three. With so many containers to juggle Matt absolutely required Anne's assistance to carry some of the items.

The overhead lights were still on when they took their seats, but their arrival had been timed so perfectly that within a few minutes the previews began to play, and very shortly after that the feature began. Anne found the first minutes of the movie very entertaining, and for one of the few times since her arrival in the States actually forgot her environment for some time as she watched. Only during the slower parts, did she occasionally glance across the small person seated at her left to glimpse Matt's striking profile as he gazed intently at the screen.

Surely it was not wrong for her to engage in a slight pretense that this was her family. Maybe pretense was all she would ever have. Well, pretending to have a family was better than never enjoying the experience of belonging to someone at all.

After a while Matt put his arm across the back of Karen's seat as if to draw the child closer to him. However, he did not cuddle the little girl. Instead, he left his arm draped across the back of her chair. For the rest of the show, Anne was conscious of his hand resting tantalizingly near her shoulder. She could almost feel the heat of it through the sheer fabric of her blouse, and if she moved only a little she could feel her shawl-collar brush across Matt's fingertips.

But in spite of being so conscious of Matt's presence, Anne couldn't help alternately laughing wholeheartedly and weeping. The movie launched an avalanche of emotions, which were perhaps engendered more by her fragile state of mind than by the talent of the actors on the screen.

When the feature ended, Anne once again escorted Karen to the loo, thereby proving the necessity of her having accompanied the two as Karen's special aide.

Anne was surprised when she found that Matt did not plan to take her directly home. The next stop was a fast food restaurant, featuring primarily fish and chips with something called hush puppies and corn on the cob as well. Anne was delighted with the fish and chips which reminded her of home but were much better as there was no greasy taste whatever. The fish was firm, yet tender, the flavor delicate.

Matt and Anne finished their meal ahead of Karen, who as Matt had mentioned on the occasion of their first meeting, was a very slow eater. She ate well, but very carefully, meticulously chewing each small bite very thoroughly before swallowing.

"Sometimes it's difficult to be patient while I wait on her," Matt commented. "It's great to have someone along to keep me company while I wait."

A few minutes later, during a lull in the conversation, Anne happened to catch the eye of a middle-aged woman at a neighboring table.

"Your little girl's mighty pretty," the woman said. Anne opened her mouth to explain that Karen was not her child but Matt slipped a reply in quickly, "Yes, indeed she is," he said. "Anne and I are very proud of her."

"You're impossible!" Anne scolded him.

Karen eventually finished her meal, but her consumption of a large glass of cola necessitated another trip to the ladies' loo before the three could leave the restaurant. Anne did not mind accompanying her at all. In fact, she enjoyed being with Karen and having the opportunity to pretend that the little girl was her own. Karen was sprightly and intelligent and so polite that it was impossible not to love her. What Anne did mind, however, was the fact that each time she accompanied the child to the rest room she was forcibly reminded of the reason she had been asked to go along on this afternoon outing.

Shortly after the three left the restaurant and began driving toward Fairfield, Karen's head slumped over as she fell sound asleep. Anne leaned across the back of the front seat and straightened the sturdy little body in her booster seat so that her head rested against the upholstered side panel of the car. She pulled the tiny feet down a little to arrange the child at an angle that would prevent her head from slumping forward again. It was difficult to put her in a comfortable position with her seat belt on; but of course it was imperative for her safety that it remain fastened.

"I don't mind the view," Matt said, with a sidewise glance at the shapely derriere presently turned foremost in the seat beside him, "But you don't need to worry about Karen. She won't be uncomfortable. When she's tired enough, she can sleep anywhere."

Anne belatedly realized the awkward position she was presently in and turned around quickly to re-seat herself. She rebuckled her seat belt with somewhat more force than was necessary in order to cover her embarrassment, then kept her face turned away from Matt's eyes. A disinterested observer would have noted instantly that her face was as red as the rosy cheeks of the child sleeping peacefully in the back seat of the automobile.

Only a slight flicker of amusement in Matt's eyes indicated that he realized that Anne had not regained her composure as easily as she had regained her seat. He watched, without appearing to do so, as she smoothed her skirts and stared fixedly out the window, avoiding his gaze.

It was a few moments before he spoke again. When he broke the silence, it was to ask, "How do you like Fairfield so far? Do you think you'll be happy here?"

Anne was instantly on guard, fearing another effort was afoot to convince her to sell her house, "I doubt you really care," she answered defensively.

"Have you any reason to doubt me?" Matt asked, turning slightly toward her in the seat. He reached out and lightly grasped her knee which lay tantalizingly near him in the adjacent bucket seat, allowing his hand to continue to lie there as he drove down the road.

Anne's impatient answer was somewhat untruthful as well. "I don't think about you one way or the other," she said.

"Then you can answer my question," he said calmly, giving her knee a gentle squeeze. "How do you like it here in Fairfield?"

"Fine," she answered automatically, in her crisp accent. By now her mind was fully occupied by the hand that seemed to be nearly burning the flesh of her knee. She knew she had given mixed signals before when she had first responded to this man's lovemaking and then resisted him. She did not want to make the same mistake twice.

When it seemed she had allowed the hand to remain on her knee for an unconscionably long time, she became desperate to take some type of action. She picked up the offending hand as if were an object she held in great distaste, moved it a few inches away from her person and allowed it to drop.

Matt merely looked at her quizzically as he replaced the hand on the steering wheel; he made no comment.

When he spoke again a few minutes later, it was to mention Anne's aunt. "I really liked and respected Agatha Brownfield," he said. "How well did you know her? Surely not too well, considering the distance..."

"Oh, but I did know her well!" Anne exclaimed; and soon she was chatting comfortably, telling about her long-standing relationship with her aunt Aggie and how the two had kept in touch over the years.

It seemed only a minute before the automobile arrived at Anne's house. Bill's old truck in the drive and a couple of lights within the house indicated that Janet and Bill had arrived back home. Because Karen was still sound asleep, Matt merely walked around the car to assist Anne as she stepped out. He did not accompany her to the door, electing instead to remain near the sleeping child.

Just as Anne placed her hand on the door handle she heard him call to her softly, "Anne." She turned and saw that he was standing on the driver's side of the car again with the door slightly open as he looked toward her. "I'll call you soon," he told her gently, just loudly enough to be heard but not loudly enough to awaken Karen.

Anne merely nodded her head. A breathless feeling compressed her chest at the personal note she heard in his voice. One instant later however, she banged the door behind her as she entered the house. *He certainly does know how to get to me,* she thought angrily. Then she went into the sitting room to visit with Bill and Janet and hear about their day.

# CHAPTER 16

The next morning Anne slipped quietly out of bed and tiptoed down the hall to the bathroom, carefully closing the door after entering so the sound of her shower would not awaken Janet. The two girls had stayed up long after Bill Rodgers had gone home, discussing a myriad of topics from gossip about other tenants in the building where they had their flat in London to the more immediate topics of Bill Rodgers and Matthew Stevens.

Anne had gotten up early because she wanted to do her housework this morning before the stone mason came to discuss Aunt Aggie's headstone; but she wanted her friend to get all the sleep she needed. She was somewhat surprised, therefore, as she stepped out of the shower, to hear an alarm clock jangling insistently in Janet's bedroom. It was unlike Janet to set an alarm for waking up anytime when she didn't absolutely have to.

As Anne toweled herself off, she heard Janet stumbling around in the bedroom; and at last the alarm clock ceased ringing. Anne stuck her head out the bathroom door.

"You're up early, aren't you, Dearie?" she called.

Janet came out of the bedroom stretching mightily. "It sure seems early," she said, "I may be dealing with jet lag, but I'm meeting Bill in the carriage house in less than an hour. He says he's nearly finished with the apartment he's building and he wants to show me what he's doing. And," she added dramatically, "I'm going to help."

"You!" Anne hooted, surveying her delicate companion with skepticism.

"I'm sure I'll enjoy it," Janet said, flapping her slippers as she passed Anne in the hall on her way to her own shower.

Anne's eyes followed in amazement as her friend entered the bathroom and shut the door. She stood a few minutes absent mindedly toweling her hair until the sound of the shower broke her reverie. *Love,* she decided, *can have an amazing effect on people.*

After Janet skipped cheerfully out to the carriage house to help Bill Rodgers, Anne did her thorough cleaning for the day, choosing to clean the powder room and clear the aged contents from its medicine cabinet, after which she vacuumed the sitting room and plumped its pillows to restore order from the disarray caused by the prior evening's visiting and snacking. Her cleaning equipment was barely put away when she heard the doorbell ring.

Mr. Bello was at the door with a tall, thin gentleman carrying a thick book and a small order pad. The stranger was Tom Selford of Selford Monuments.

"How do you do," Mr. Selford said to Anne as she held out her hand to accept his handshake. His voice was very deep and grave, quite befitting his profession.

Anne led the two gentlemen into the sun room where she seated them at the round oak table and offered them refreshment of tea or lemonade. When they declined the offer, Anne sat down at the table herself and began looking at the pictured designs in Mr. Selford's book.

It did not take her long to locate the stone she desired. When she explained to Mr. Selford that she wanted one exactly like her uncle's except for the color, he confirmed that the stone she had chosen was a twin to the major's. He had himself sold Agatha Brownfield her husband's stone and he remembered it well.

When Anne explained that she would like the style of lettering to be the same as well, Mr. Selford promised to consult the previous order information to match the style exactly.

Anne had already written out the wording of the inscription; so after a few minutes scribbling in his note pad, Mr. Selford was able to set a price for the stone. Fifty percent was to be paid in advance. Anne would have an opportunity to approve the stone when it was finished and would then pay the remaining fifty percent before the stone was placed on Aggie's grave.

Anne carefully wrote out the cheque for the deposit amount—nearly all she had earned at her yard sale. Doing so gave her great satisfaction. Aunt Aggie's name would be carved in the stone in clear, deep letters which would be almost a metaphor for the simplicity and strength of Aggie herself. Anne knew that in placing the order with Mr. Selford she had completed an important step in her recovery from grief.

Mr. Selford had followed Mr. Bello to Anne's house in his own vehicle; and after he left, Mr. Bello stayed a few more minutes, chatting with Anne on the wide front porch. He had news to tell because he had just learned that the financing had been successfully arranged through the local bank to enable his son to locate his factory, Novelties, Inc., at the chosen site in Fairfield. Anthony and his wife and little Vickie Ann would definitely be returning to live in Fairfield permanently.

"Mama is so excited!" he exclaimed, causing Anne to smile inwardly because she doubted that woman was any more excited than her obviously delighted husband.

Just as Mr. Bello started down the steps to take his leave, a small blue automobile pulled into the drive. Anne was instantly annoyed when she saw that it bore the insignia of the Fairfield Realty Company. She steeled herself to endure another pitched effort to convince her to part with Aunt Aggie's house.

When an impossibly large man emerged from the small blue car, Mr. Bello rushed forward to meet him, fairly bubbling with enthusiasm.

"Mr. Thomas, how nice to see you! My boy's gonna look you up later on today. He's moving home and he needs a house. You sell him one right in this neighborhood, you hear. Mama and I want to see our granddaughter every day." He nearly pumped Mr. Thomas's arm off before leading him to the porch where Anne waited. His face was jovial as he presented the newcomer.

"Anne," Mr. Bello said, "This is Mr. Thomas, the best real estate agent in..." At that moment something in Anne's face caused him to falter.

In the silence that followed, Anne spoke directly to the newcomer. "Mr. Thomas, this house is not for sale. I have told Matt Stevens repeatedly it is not for sale. You're wasting your time here." As usual, when Anne became excited her words were spoken in an even more precise and clipped fashion than usual. At this moment, although she was standing perfectly still in a proud, upright stance, she appeared to fairly bristle with suppressed resentment and her accent was almost too British to be understood by the American ears of her two listeners.

Mr. Thomas was not easily daunted. Skirting the subject of the house for the time being, he stretched out his hand in greeting, saying as he did, "Miss. Long, how nice to finally meet you. I see the tales of your beauty have not been exaggerated."

"Oh, no indeed," Mr. Bello said, his face creasing in its familiar smile as he too attempted to skirt the awkwardness of Anne's displeasure. "Anne's just as pretty as all the young men in town are saying.

"My boy will look you up this afternoon, Mr. Thomas," he added; and then with a nod to Thomas and a wink of his eye toward Anne, Mr. Bello departed.

"This is a lovely house," Mr. Thomas said, eyeing the graceful columns of the front porch and patting one of them with the outstretched hand which Anne had ignored. They don't build them like this anymore. I can see why you want to keep it, if you can."

"For the time being, I *can*," Anne said stiffly.

"Matt Stevens told me how you feel," Mr. Thomas said gently. "However, before we knew you would want to come here to live, a generous offer was made for this house. The offer has now been increased by more than half again what was originally offered.

"Truthfully," he said with a sigh, "I tried to talk the buyer out of making the new offer. It's more than the house is worth."

"The amount offered is of no consequence to me," Anne told him. "The house is simply not for sale."

"It's your house; you can do what you want with it," Mr. Thomas told her gently, "But why don't you at least take this proposal. The buyer has indicated he will be willing to wait as long as necessary for this house. If you change your mind about selling later, you may be interested in the offer." Thomas handed Anne a sealed envelope, which she accepted silently.

Mr. Thomas gave her a long sympathetic look and offered his hand again as he said, "I've enjoyed this opportunity to meet you, Miss Long. Please don't hold my errand against me."

This time Anne shook hands with him willingly, for in truth she could not hold his position as intermediary against him, as she knew he had approached her in the line of duty under Matt Stevens' orders. He was a warm, teddy bear type of man wearing a well-worn, brown suit which seemed as much a part of him as the salt and pepper gray of his hair. Anne found herself reluctantly liking him and almost regretting that he would not be earning a commission from the sale of her house; but she did not invite him to come in and with no encouragement to tarry, he soon departed.

When he had gone, Anne went back into the house and into the sun room where she picked up the duplicate of the order for Aunt Aggie's memorial from the round oak table where it had been left. She carried it to the secretary in the small sitting room off the kitchen. When she stuffed the order into one of the pigeon holes, she put the sealed envelope containing the offer for her house into the pigeon hole along with it, unopened.

*"I will not sell Aunt Aggie's house"* she vowed silently.

A few minutes later, she went down the back porch steps on her way to the carriage house to check on how the apartment was coming. She was surprised to see that, for the first time since her arrival, the garage door of the building was open wide. Not only that, but a good-sized truck was backed nearly into the garage. As she watched, Bill and another young man came out of the building carrying pieces of lumber.

# CHAPTER 17

"Hi, Anne," Bill called cheerfully. "I hope you don't mind that I asked the lumber yard to come pick this stuff up. I'm almost finished and I don't need the rest of this lumber."

"It's fine," she answered as she walked across the lawn. "I want to bring Aunt Aggie's car home anyway, and I need space for it."

"The lumber yard is giving me a receipt for the lumber you return today, Anne." Bill told her. "After they figure up what it's worth, they'll pay for it; although unfortunately you won't get the cash. They'll have to send a check to Agatha's estate, but I guess you'll get the money in the long run."

"By the way," he said, nodding toward a tin container at the foot of the steps. "This fella showed up just when I was about to take that paint thinner up to Janet. Maybe you could take it up to her."

Anne picked up the can and ran up the stairs. In the small bathroom of the flat she found Janet, up to her elbows in water in the tiny lavatory.

"Don't laugh," she said immediately when Anne entered. She turned her face toward the doorway and Anne saw that it was covered with splotches of a gooey, gray-colored substance. "This water isn't taking it off at all. I hope the paint thinner will work." She pulled her arms, liberally coated with the same substance, as were her clothes, out of the water and dried them on an old rag.

"What in the world is it?" Anne asked.

"Rubber cement," Janet said. "We just finished installing this *wretched* floor. Bill didn't get a speck on him, but just look at me!"

At her impassioned remark, Anne, who had not previously felt the situation humorous, abruptly felt otherwise and laughed delightedly. "Well, the floor looks great at any rate," she said to her friend, as she looked at the tile's bright, white background with its marbled blue pattern, "But we wouldn't want to spill the paint thinner on it and ruin it. Come downstairs and out of doors and I'll help you get that stuff off."

Stopping only to pick up a few rags from Bill's supply, the two young women went downstairs just as the boy from the lumberyard slammed shut the tailgate of the truck. Bill joined them at the picnic table where Anne painstakingly soaked the rubbery goo from her friend's forearms while he removed the smaller spots from her face, taking infinite care to keep the paint thinner well away from her eyes. When most of the glue had been removed, Bill unrolled the garden hose from its storage reel alongside the carriage house and rinsed Janet's skin to remove all traces of the solvent.

Soon the two were taking turns squirting one another with the hose; and when Anne got caught in the overspray she joined the play as well, grabbing the hose Bill had dropped before Janet could pick it up and chasing Bill across the lawn with it until it's spray hit the gleaming finish of a small car she had not noticed pulling into the drive.

Anne stopped dead in her tracks, holding the nozzle of the hose limply at her side, allowing the spray to fall harmlessly on a nearby bush. She was aware that her tee shirt was soaking wet and plastered to her body and that within her tennis shoes her toes were squishing in small pools of water. Feeling distinctly uncomfortable, she tugged at the shirt to loosen it from her skin.

Taking in the situation at a glance, Bill walked to the faucet and turned it off. When the water ceased spraying, the door to the small sports car opened and Matt Stevens emerged.

"I take it that it's safe to get out now," he commented, eyeing the water splotches on the hood of his vehicle with no evidence of good humor.

"I've disarmed her," Bill chuckled as he strolled carelessly back across the lawn.

"None too soon, I see," Matt said, his eyes on Bill's dripping clothing.

"It was two against one," Bill said nonchalantly, giving no clue that Anne had been late to enter the fray.

Regaining her wits at last, Anne introduced Matt to Janet, who in her state of dishabille came somewhat reluctantly across the grass when she was beckoned. "This is my visitor from England, Janet Conard," Anne said. "You can see you caught us somewhat off guard. Janet, this is Matt Stevens, the attorney who is handling Aunt Aggie's estate."

"I had hoped I could ask the two of you a favor," Matt replied somewhat doubtfully as be offered his hand to Janet. "My secretary reminded me today that kindergarten starts in a few weeks. Karen needs new clothes. The housekeeper is hopeless. She would dress the child entirely in long dresses with white aprons if it was up to her, and she complains that I buy Karen nothing but blue jeans and tee shirts. I wondered if you two could go with me to the City South Mall and help me choose an appropriate wardrobe." He spread his hands in a helpless fashion as if a child's wearing apparel was an unfathomable mystery to him.

Anne looked at Janet for a clue as to what her answer should be. Not surprisingly, a small gleam had begun in Janet's eyes at the thought of shopping. Anne was herself enticed by the idea of choosing clothing that would complement the small, yet sturdy frame of the moppet she was rapidly growing to love. It would be terrible if Karen were to start school in clothing in which she was uncomfortable or felt out of place.

"When do you want us to go?" she asked Matt with simple directness.

"Can we go this afternoon?" he asked. "Karen has been home all morning. She slept late and is well-rested so she should be able to stand up to trying a few things on, if you ladies can get ready in a short while, that is; I mean if you don't have anything planned." He looked back and forth from Anne and Janet, who looked as if they might take some time to get themselves back in order, to Bill, as if wondering if the red-headed carpenter could spare the companionship of the two young women.

"We'll manage if you give us an hour and a half," Janet answered. "It will be a pleasure," she added, already anticipating the joy of visiting an American mall.

"Don't worry about me," Bill said evenly. "I planned to wind up a few things in the apartment over the next few days and I have no time to waste."

"Well, if it's okay, I'll be back later to pick you up," Matt said to the girls, before sliding back into his car and driving away.

"When he comes back, you might ask him if I can pick the car up for you tomorrow," Bill told Anne. "The license branch is open every week-day. I think it's time you took that test and I start teaching you to drive."

"Come on in for a few minutes, Bill," Anne said. "I wouldn't want to delay Matt Stevens, but it's time for lunch. I don't want to shop on an empty stomach."

Matt, stopped at a stop sign a block away, was able to see Bill in his rearview mirror as the two girls entering the house while he held the door for them. When traffic cleared, Matt turned northward, entering the street with somewhat more acceleration than was actually required.

By the time Matt returned with Karen, both Anne and Janet had redone their water-soaked hair and were dressed in slim slacks and crisp blouses suitable for the planned shopping excursion. Anne's blouse was cream-colored with an embroidered design of orange-colored thread on the breast pocket which set off her flaming hair. Janet's blouse, like most of her clothing, was crimson. The two made an arresting sight as they exited the house and joined Karen and Matt at the side door where Matt had rung the bell. They bore little resemblance to the two disheveled young women Matt had seen a scant ninety minutes earlier.

"I see you're ready," he commented with a hint of humor in his voice.

"Anne, I get to buy new clothes for school," Karen was hopping eagerly up and down as she spoke.

"So you do," Anne replied. "Tell me what kind of clothes you like best." With her ready rapport for the little girl she was so absorbed in the child that almost without thinking she climbed into the back seat with her to continue her conversation.

"Wouldn't you rather get in front, Anne?" Janet asked, hesitating before entering the vehicle.

"Not really," Anne told her. "I get nervous watching the traffic fly by on the wrong side. I'll just keep Karen company."

If Matt was unhappy regarding the seating arrangements, he gave no sign as he closed the passenger door and returned to his own seat. He and Janet conversed like old friends all the way to the mall, which was the same shopping center he and Anne and Karen had visited the previous day to attend the movie.

# CHAPTER 18

"Can we get everything she needs in one trip?" Matt asked as they entered the enormous main doors of the shopping plaza. He was speaking to Anne, who was holding tightly to Karen's hand. Janet, as if smelling the scent of new clothing, had already advanced several yards ahead of the others.

"With Janet along you can outfit her twice over in half a day," Anne answered. "She's an all-time shopping champ."

Soon the three females were deep in the clothing racks of little girls' clothing in a major department store.

"We must buy trendy things," Janet whispered. "The younger children are, the quicker they embrace new things." She pulled several items off the rack to briefly inspect them before putting them back. The first things to meet her approval turned out to be mix and match outfits of tops, little skirts with shorts attached beneath and leggings, each comprised of several bright colors. While each had a single dominant color, all could be combined with one another because the other colors were used as trim.

"These are darling." Janet said.

Anne agreed that the clothing was attractive, but thinking of the child's need to be independent, quickly steered Janet away from items that fastened up the back or had too many buttons. The outfits the two women finally suggested Karen try on were of similar brightly colored patterns but were made of wash and wear knitted fabric and featured only decorative, non-functioning buttons.

In reality the tops were tee-shirts, but were made feminine by the addition of a row of ruffles at the shoulders and around the hem. They could be paired with tights, leggings of a dozen solid colors or even jeans. The style suited the slender build of the child to perfection, and Matt would have bought them in all the colors available had not Anne raised an eyebrow and reminded him that a little girl would not want all her clothes to be identical.

Thus chastened, Matt bought only a few of the delightful tops and allowed Karen to choose the colors of several pairs of tights and a couple of leggings, which he also bought before the shopping was continued at another store.

At the next store they found slightly longer, dress-length jumper tops of the same knitted fabric. These could be paired with long or short-sleeve tee shirts depending on the weather and were long enough to be worn with ankle socks as well as with tights. Matt cast the deciding vote on what colors would be purchased, after which Janet and Anne chose tee shirts and ankle socks to match and coordinate with the colors chosen. In the same shop, Anne spoke a quiet word to Matt, after which he left her alone to help the child choose a supply of tiny panties and undershirts, with Matt returning only to pay for the items chosen.

Their next stop was at a children's shoe store where tiny sneakers, ornamented with cartoon characters and fastened with Velcro straps, were purchased at a price which made Anne blanch.

At Matt's prodding, the clerk also brought out lined boots for winter days, and tiny red patent slippers for Sundays.

With the latter on her feet, Karen pirouetted around the store, scarcely able to contain her pleasure.

"Thank you, Daddy. I love everything," she said running to hug Matt who was seated in one of a row of chairs where her shoes had been fitted. "And thank you, Anne," she said turning to Anne who was standing nearby. She then hugged Anne with such enthusiasm that Anne could barely maintain her balance. "Daddy never bought me such neat things before."

"Men don't always know what girls like," Anne told her. "Pretty soon, though, you'll be able to choose for yourself."

"But you'll always help me, won't you Anne," the child said artlessly.

With Matt's eyes on her and the child's eyes beseeching her, Anne chose her words carefully. "Whenever your father asks me to help, I'll do what I can," she said gently, before suggesting that Karen put her old shoes back on so they could leave the store.

"Let her wear the new ones home," Matt growled. "There aren't enough Sundays for her to wear them out before she outgrows them anyway."

And so the three adults, burdened with packages, left the store a few steps behind the child, who trip-trapped along in prideful consciousness of her new red slippers, which looked, she said, like Dorothy's ruby slippers in "The Wizard of Oz".

"Don't forget to ask Matt about the car," Janet reminded Anne, as she eyed window after window of beautiful clothing. "I know how to drive, and I want to come here again."

"The paper work is all ready for you to sign, Anne," Matt said. "Pick the car up whenever you like, but you probably should see Mr. Thomas at the real estate office before you do. He handles automobile insurance and you need it to legally drive the car."

"Thank you, I'll take care of everything tomorrow," Anne said, wondering as she spoke how much the car insurance would cost.

"Karen, stop a minute. Let's go in this shop." Matt said. Taking the child by the hand he entered a nearby young women's apparel shop which had elaborate displays of casual and sports clothing. He stopped before a display of slim ladies' trousers with sweater tops of wide ribbed knit. The two girls, lagging behind to look at other items on display did not hear what he said to the clerk, but they did notice her looking them up and down before taking two of the pants sets off the rack, one in deep brick red, the other in russet.

"We'll take them," Matt said, handing the clerk a credit card from his wallet.

"Matt, we couldn't accept them," Anne said as she understood what he was doing.

"It's a thank you gift and you must accept," Matt said firmly, and then, stepping closer to Anne, he leaned toward her and whispered quickly in her ear, "Besides, I couldn't stand the hungry look in Janet's eyes anymore."

"She has that effect on people," Anne replied as she watched her friend hold up another of the brick red sweater and pants suits admiringly. "I think you've chosen her gift well," Anne added. "She loves it."

"However," Matt told her, "I chose to buy the pant suits because the other one is so perfect for you. In the fall, the leaves in the countryside will be golden and russet with touches of red. You will blend right in and be more gorgeous than the sugar maples."

It was impossible to know if Matt meant the remark as a serious compliment or was merely teasing her, so Anne made no response; and the moment passed as he stepped forward to sign the charge slip prepared by the clerk.

"Now let's go eat," he said as he shifted packages in his arms to accept the sleek mauve bag the clerk handed him. "I'm starved."

"Can you carry this package, Anne?" he added. "It's one too many for me."

"It's the least I can do," she answered, thinking of the price she had seen on the rack holding the pant suits. She and Janet rearranged their parcels; and somehow, among the three adults, everything was carried to the tiny sports car, where it was soon stuffed into the trunk.

Dinner was at a child-themed restaurant, surrounded by a miniature golf course. "Karen's favorite place to eat," Matt whispered.

After the meal, to Karen's delight, Matt insisted they play a round of golf and he would have gone round the course yet again had not Anne begged for mercy.

In the short trip from mall to restaurant Anne had found herself seated beside Matt; but now, once again, she sat in back with Karen. The child soon snuggled down in her seat to quickly fall asleep. How right it feels to be with her, Anne thought. Then she listened to Janet's happy chatter from the front seat until she drifted to sleep as well.

It seemed only a moment before she stumbled out of the car in her own driveway. Matt handed her the mauve-colored sack and took the key from her hand to unlock the door for her. "You're pretty tired, aren't you?" he asked kindly.

"I get up early every morning. There's so much I want to do in the house before I find a job."

"Sleep late tomorrow," he advised gruffly, looking at her sleepy eyes as Janet slipped in the door ahead of them. He lifted Anne's chin a little. "Taking care of this big house would wear anyone out."

"I don't mind," Anne snapped, jerking away from his hand. "It's worth the effort!"

Matt stopped her with a hand on her shoulder. "The house becomes you Anne. I think you do belong here, but I know as you cannot how difficult it will be to maintain it. I still think you should sell it because then you would have the money to live somewhere else in comfort. It would be foolish to live here until you can no longer afford it and you lose everything; but there's no hurry about changing your mind. As long as you stay here I hope we'll be friends. Karen loves you, you know."

Anne dropped her head, "Please don't mention selling the house to me again," she begged. "I know you're telling me the truth but I can't think about it right now. It's too soon."

"Poor Baby," Matt said, drawing her to him and cuddling her beneath his chin. "It must be difficult being here without Aggie." He held her, stroking her hair with one hand until she became conscious of the steady, soothing throb of his heart beat. A moment later he stepped away from her because he would not risk having her once again misconstrue his actions; but all Anne understood as his car drove away was that, having been thrust from the cradle of his embrace, she felt bereft.

# CHAPTER 19

Anne had been stirred by his touch—deeply stirred, into the depths of her being. As she followed her friend's footsteps into the house, she shook her head slightly as she sought to understand her own heart. Why was it that after years of dating the boys and men of her home country and walking away unmoved, this man—this one man in the small town of Fairfield was the one who could touch her inner self? How strange love was when it came calling. She had not previously been in love, but this surely must be it—the bright, fresh, new beginnings of it.

She said goodnight to Janet who had stopped in the kitchen to fix herself a "cuppa" and dreamily climbed the elegant staircase to the upper hall and a night of ceaseless dreaming of a sweet future that included a man by her side that cared for her and a small hand resting trustingly in hers.

The dream was shattered the next morning when, buoyed by a night of the sweet dreams, she began a task she had here-to-fore delayed, the clearing of her aunt's small rosewood secretary desk which was located in the tiny bay window of the little sitting room. When she had previously given the room a thorough cleaning, Anne had polished its satiny exterior and had peered into its carefully arranged cubbies and drawers; but she had not disturbed any of the documents carefully folded away.

Now, with the tiny bud of hope for the future nestled in her heart, it seemed easier to delve into the remnants of her aunt's past. She pulled a small chair with a delicately curved back and a needlepoint seat of deep burgundy roses up to the secretary and pulled out the sliding shelf which served as a work surface.

Half an hour later she was lost in deep thought, the cold chill of suspicion settling into her heart as she set aside her foolish dreams. She was once again sure she meant nothing to

Matt. It was only the house he cared for. He'd probably do anything to acquire it.

She went into the hall to look up the number in order to phone Mr. Thomas at his agency. It was time for her to bring the car home. She needed desperately to become independent of Mr. Matt Stevens.

When Mr. Thomas questioned her about the make and model of the car, she could supply no answer except that the car was five years old. Mr. Thomas had insured the car for Agatha, however; so he was able to look up the information in his records and give Anne the amount of the insurance premium. It would make a large hole in her resources; but Anne realized that without the car it would be difficult for her to ever find a job; and it was becoming increasingly clear that she not only had to have a job, but that she had to have one right away.

While Anne waited for Bill to show up at the carriage house so she could ask him to pick up the car, she decided to make good use of her time. When Janet came downstairs a few minutes later she found Anne in the sitting room studying the driver's manual.

Taking the thick pamphlet from her friend's knee, Janet commented, "It looks as if there's a lot to learn here. How are you doing?"

"I think I'm ready," Anne said. "I've studied for days. Right now I'm asking myself the sample questions in the back."

"Come in the kitchen and I'll help," Janet told her.

The two settled themselves at the kitchen table with cups of tea, a packet of muffins and jam. For the next hour Janet asked Anne questions from the back of the book. At the end of that time she agreed that Anne was as prepared as possible for taking the test for her driver's permit.

By early afternoon, Aunt Aggie's dark blue sedan was parked in the curved drive near the side door of the house. Bill had walked to town and picked it up at mid-morning and then taken Anne to the local license bureau branch where she had passed her exam with flying colors. With the new permit safely stowed in her wallet she was ready for her first driving lesson.

Janet and Bill had just come back from the apartment where Bill had been showing off his latest plumbing efforts and were bickering amiably about who would supervise Anne's first driving lesson when the phone rang.

Anne picked up the phone and answered in her usual, clear businesslike manner. "Good afternoon, this is Anne Long."

Janet noticed that her knuckles grew white as she gripped the phone and told the caller, "Actually I do have plans. I'm planning to dine with friends this evening." Her voice was decidedly cool.

Janet watched closely as her friend continued speaking into the receiver, "Yes, you may ask again, but I'm not likely to be available. I'm planning to get a job, you know."

A few seconds later Anne continued in a slightly sharper tone, "Yes, I am still planning to keep this house. I know that must disappoint you but after all, it is *my house.*"

Then the closing remark, delivered in an airy fashion, "I'm sure I won't need any further help. Don't be concerned about me at all." Followed by, "Yes, good-bye then."

"Was that Matt Stevens you talked to that way?" Janet asked bluntly.

"Yes, as a matter of fact it was."

"But Anne, I was sure you *liked* Mr. Stevens," Janet said. "Why ever were you so stuffy with him?" she questioned.

Her friend's reply was only a grim look.

Janet and Bill shrugged their shoulders and shook their heads behind her back before following Anne out the door for her driving lesson.

Downtown, in Matt Stevens' office, the bewildered attorney was still holding the treacherous telephone in his hand, looking at it in dismay. Anne Long had brushed him off, and from the sound of her she had somehow taken a definite dislike to him. "What on earth did I do wrong?" he asked himself before slowly replacing the phone in its cradle and returning to the never-ending pile of papers on his desk.

Bill had driven the two young women to a nearly deserted country road far outside the limits of Fairfield when Ann slid into the driver's seat for a nerve-wracking first driving lesson, made more nerve wracking by the fact that she was now driving from the side of the vehicle where for a lifetime she had been seated as a passenger.

"Driving," Bill assured her, "Will soon be second nature to you," but for now even being behind the wheel was an alien experience for Anne. Never-the-less, with determination born of necessity, she practiced for more than an hour with attempts at making smooth stops and starts.

"Pretend there is an egg between your foot and the petro peddle," Janet advised from the back seat after one precipitous start.

"Anticipate what's coming up," Bill told her when she stopped far too quickly. "Give yourself plenty of time to slow down gradually."

Finally, miraculously, she began to catch on to how it was done and her passengers were able to relax and breathe a little easier.

"This lesson is officially over," Bill said a while later. "You've worked hard enough for one day and you're doing great. We'll come back out again in a few days and practice cornering. It'll be thirty days before you're allowed to apply for your license anyway, and you'll be ready far sooner than that."

"I have to be," Anne said firmly. "I have to find a job before I run out of funds."

After parking near the garage, Bill walked around the car and slung his arms across the shoulders of each of his companions.

"So," he said, "How do you two feel about Pizza tonight?"

"Pizza?" Janet asked.

"You've never had pizza like Dino's makes it," Bill said. "You'll love it."

"You two go ahead," Anne told them. "I have other plans."

"What other plans?" Janet asked, suspiciously."When you told Matt you were going out with friends, I thought you meant us."

"I did," Anne admitted, "But now I just want to stay home and relax. You go with Bill. This is your vacation. You should be having fun."

Late that afternoon, after her friends had reluctantly left for dinner, promising to bring her take-out later, Anne went into the little sitting room and sank wearily onto the sofa. The secretary writing shelf was still pulled out just as she had left it early in the morning. She gazed at the dull, burgundy red leather of Aunt Aggie's journal resting on its surface. Finally she stood and picked up the book, put the small desk chair back in position against the wall and closed up the desk. She carried the book back to the sofa with her, switching on the reading lamp before she sat down.

After she opened the book to the same page where she had closed it earlier in the day, she found herself once again staring at the same page, unable to turn it to read further. Aunt Aggie's words told her too clearly exactly what interest she held for Matt Stevens.

There in her precise, easy-to-read script she had written about Matt Stevens' compelling interest in buying her house. He had come to her "out of the blue" to inquire if she might consider selling it. It seemed like he'd be willing to "give the moon" for it if necessary. Aunt Aggie admitted that she had taken quite a liking to the "young fellow" but she had no intention of selling. The house she had written, underlining it twice, had been too long without a family. She hoped she would live to see her dear niece married and raising children here. The apartment would become her own quarters, and at last the family she had always wanted would fill the rooms of her lonely old house.

*After Aunt Aggie died Matt must have thought it would not be necessary to 'give the moon' to acquire the house,* Anne thought. He must have assumed it would be his for the asking. How dare him try to convince her she should sell the house for her own best interests! It was his interests he was concerned about. *Matt Stevens was—to express it in just one word—a phony!*

Anne slammed the journal shut once more and tossed it toward the end of the sofa. She then switched on the television set and glumly *did not* watch it until she finally dozed off. "I will never sell this house," she told herself firmly just before drifting into sleep.

# CHAPTER 20

When Anne awoke with a start, wondering just what it was that had wakened her, she heard the old hall clock chime one time. Glancing across at the small brass clock on the secretary she noted that it was now seven o'clock. Apparently she was growing used to the sound of the striking gong, far louder here than was audible in her bedroom, for she had slept through six of the gongs before she had awakened.

But perhaps it was not the gong that had awakened her. She was famished! Now that hunger had attacked her, she realized that she had skipped breakfast altogether and only nibbled at cheese and crackers at lunch time. Bill and Janet would probably bring her some pizza later, but she was hungry *now.* She needed a meal.

In the little kitchen she found a tin of soup and started warming it in a pan. In the 'fridge she located some crisp carrots to munch as she set out a bowl for her soup and a single spoon. It made a lonely place setting.

When her soup began to bubble slightly, she turned off the burner and went to the front of the house to look on the porch for her newspaper. After bringing it inside, she spread it across the emptiness of the table before tasting the first bite of the surprisingly good chicken soup. When she turned her attention to the paper, a bold headline caught her eye, *"Stevens will Moderate Meeting."*

She read the first paragraph with avid interest:

*"A groundswell of public opinion against the planned factory in the newly zoned industrial complex at the north edge of town continues to grow. With the planned protest meeting now only one week away, supporters of the factory face an uphill battle to convince those who believe the factory will destroy the integrity of the north road area, which up to this time has been exclusively*

111

*residential. Matt Stevens, prominent local attorney has agreed to moderate the meeting but has not publicly stated his position.*"

"I certainly plan to attend that meeting," Anne told herself "It should be very interesting."

Just then she heard the sound of Bill's old truck in the drive. Almost immediately he and Janet rushed into the kitchen, Bill balancing a large white square box on one hand held just above his head.

"Stop with the soup already," he exclaimed. "Here's your supper, and" he paused slightly for effect, "I have some *great news for you!*"

Soon Anne was caught up in the excitement of her friends. It seemed Anthony Bello, Mr. Bello's son, was the power behind the new factory which was to come to Fairfield. He needed a secretary at once to prepare a response to the objections to be put forth at the protest meeting. There was no time to be wasted in looking for someone. Mr. Thomas, of the realty and insurance office, had loaned him a computer and an office. He wanted to get started at once, the following morning.

Bill and Janet had run into the Bello family at Dino's and heard about the immediate need, and Bill had suggested Anne for the position. "Mr. Bello thought you'd be wonderful for it; and although Anthony is slightly less enthusiastic, he'll know how lucky he is as soon as he meets you.

"So," Bill concluded, "Anthony Bello will be calling you in just about one half hour. If you want the job, it's yours; and of course, although it's only temporary right now, it could lead to something permanent if he succeeds in getting the factory past the protest." Then as an afterthought, he asked. "You can use a computer, can't you?"

"Of course I can," Anne replied, "But it's possible they may use different programming here than what I have been using in England."

"Whew!" Bill said with relief "As long as you've had experience, you'll manage. This will just be word processing which is the easiest thing in the world, and Mr. Thomas's secretary will be there to get you over any rough spots. You'll do fine," he concluded, just as the phone in the sitting room began to ring.

"Good evening," she answered. "Anne Long speaking"

"Anne, this is Matt."

She heard the rich tones of his voice and swayed slightly at the pain of her intense caring. "I've just finished a late night here at the office and it's nearly Karen's bedtime already. I won't be able to see her at all this evening," he continued with regret in his voice, "So I thought I'd drive into the city and get a decent meal. I know by now you've already eaten but would you like to go along, just for the ride?"

"I'm sorry, Mr. Stevens," she said with all the coolness she could muster. "I told you I was spending this evening with friends, and actually I must hang up at once. I'm expecting an important phone call."

"Can I call you again, then?"

"I'm going to be very busy."

"What's wrong, Anne?"

"Nothing, Mr. Stevens; but I really must hang up so my other call can come through."

Matt found himself once more holding an unresponsive telephone receiver in his hand as he repeated to himself, slowly. "Mr. Stevens...Mr. Stevens," before replacing the phone in its cradle.

Anne barely had time to hang up her phone before it rang again. This time it *was* Anthony Bello. He arranged to give her a trial the following day and she promised to arrive promptly at nine o'clock at Mr. Thomas's office; but after hanging up, she went back to the kitchen and with some dismay spoke to her friend. "Janet, will you mind very much if I start this job while you're here? I do hate to leave you on your own."

113

"I'll take good care of her," Bill said with a wink. "Just sit down and eat some pizza. It's almost bedtime for a working girl."

The next morning Anne slipped out the side door of her house, leaving Janet still sleeping peacefully in the guest room. She was dressed in a cool, cream-colored sheathe, sneakers on her feet for the walk to town and conservative dress pumps and pocket book in her carry-all net shopping bag. At the last minute she had added an umbrella to the bag as the sky looked slightly overcast; but by the time she had reached Mr. Thomas's office, the early morning sun had broken through the cloud cover and she had begun to feel uncomfortably warm.

She was surprised upon entering the cool interior of the realty office to discover that the office building, nondescript on the exterior, was tastefully decorated in tones of the palest muted sage and cream with deep forest green carpeting. The woodwork was of a warm, honey pine and the total effect was very restful and pleasant. Mr. Thomas's secretary was busy starting a pot of coffee on a sideboard in the large front office.

"Can I help you?" she asked, turning toward Anne.

"I'm here to work for Mr. Bello," Anne told her. "Do you know where I'm supposed to report?"

"We've got an office cleared out for him to work in," the attractive middle-aged secretary said with a smile, nodding her head toward a hallway with several open doors up and down its length. "But he's not here yet so you might as well have a donut and some coffee.

"My name's Margaret," she said extending her hand, "And you must be Anne Long. I'd wager you're the only girl in this town with that accent."

"You'd be wrong right now," Anne told her, relieved to discover how much she liked the friendly woman whose help she was sure she would have to depend upon. "Right now I have a houseguest, also from England."

114

"If she's as pretty as you are, the girls in this town will be taking up a collection to send the two of you back," Margaret commented.

At that moment the door opened and Mr. Thomas walked in, accompanied by someone Anne knew instantly was Anthony Bello, for he looked exactly as his father would have looked had that gentleman been twenty-five years younger and about two stone lighter. She realized at once that he was the man who had seemed familiar when she first saw him at Stella's Cafe.

"Good morning," she said, extending her hand toward the stranger, "I'm Anne Long, and I believe we met previously."

"Yes, of course, I remember you now! I'm Anthony Bello," he told her, "And I'm afraid I'm going to work you pretty hard over the next few days."

"I'm looking forward to it," she answered, as she returned the firm hand shake he offered her. "Let's get started."

"Oh, no you don't!" Margaret said. "You've got time for a cup of coffee first; it's not nine yet."

An hour later, Anne was deep into the duties Mr. Bello had outlined for her.

First she was to make a telephone survey to discover the most common concerns of local homeowners and businesses regarding the prospect of the new factory. These were to be ranked in order of frequency. Eventually, she would be typing the list into a computer program that would feed the image to a projector so that it could be viewed by the audience on a large screen.

Mr. Bello would draft answers to the issues brought up by the townspeople and those would also be prepared to be shown to the audience at the meeting. It was his hope by this means to anticipate all of the comments that might be brought up and have his response to them already prepared.

The calls for the survey turned out to be surprisingly tedious to complete. Mr. Bello had instructed her to call two homes for each

115

single call to a business, tracking the replies on separate sheets of paper. She soon found that all of the calls were difficult, but the ones to homeowners were most difficult by far. There was no trouble picking names from the small Fairfield directory which belonged to people who lived in the north side area on any one of several streets she was surveying. The problem was that at each household she called there were more questions asked of her about her unusual accent than she was able to ask for her survey. Never-the-less, by early afternoon she had compiled a list of various concerns that had been repeated enough times to show that they would be the target items Anthony Bello would need to respond to at the meeting.

She had begun to type a list ranking the items and indicating the number of times each had been mentioned when she heard a familiar voice through the open door of the room where she was working. Matt Stevens was in the building, calling upon Mr. Thomas in an office not ten feet down the hall. She felt her heart lurch and begin to beat faster as she heard his first words.

"I'm here to talk about the offer I made on that property," he said after a few short words of greeting.

"Shhh, she'll hear you, she's in the next..." and then Mr. Thomas's door closed and Anne heard no more.

Her head swirled with fury. Well, the cat's out of the bag anyway, thanks to Aunt Aggie's journal, she thought. Matt wanted to buy the house even when Aunt Aggie was alive and he thought when she was gone he would get it. Her fingers beat a staccato rhythm against the computer keys. Then when I wouldn't sell the house to him either, he made an *anonymous* offer he thought no one could refuse. *What's the matter with that man*, she fumed. *Doesn't he know what 'no' means?*

# CHAPTER 21

Anne quickly fell into the routine of having a job again; and thankfully, this job was far more pleasant than the one she had held in London working for the two stuffy Mr. Garolds.

Mr. Bello was busy with so many things that he had only brief periods in which to offer instruction. For the most part, Anne was left on her own to complete her tasks in whatever order she preferred. A couple of times a day, Margaret would come down the hall and insist that she stop for a cup of coffee and a biscuit—referred to by Margaret as a cookie—or a soft, fragrant donut. At lunch time, Margaret insisted she accompany her to the little cafe for lunch. There she grew used to watching Stella and her waitresses bustle around while trading wisecracks with the regular customers.

Feeling that riding the bicycle would be undignified, she continued to walk to work each morning. At quitting time, Bill and Janet would arrive to pick her up, some days in Bill's old truck, other days bringing Aunt Aggie's car so Anne could have a half hour or hour's driving lesson before dinner time.

Anne enjoyed the work she was doing and her driving skills were improving daily. If she had not been feeling blue and irritated by Matt Steven's attempts to talk her into parting with her house, she would have been happier than at any previous time of her life.

One morning when Anne arrived at the office a few minutes early, as was her usual habit, she discovered Margaret and Anthony Bello drinking coffee with a newcomer, a man of large stature with twinkling gray eyes and a bushy, rust-colored beard.

"This is Jack Carter," Mr. Bello told Anne, "Jack, meet Anne, the best secretary any man ever acquired out of thin air," He snapped his fingers in demonstration of the ease at which his secretary had been acquired.

"Ah yes, you mentioned her earlier," Jack said, taking Anne's hand in his as she reached out to accept his handshake. Her slender fingers were completely engulfed, swallowed up in the huge paw he proffered.

"How do you do, Mr. Carter," Anne murmured.

"Jack is the contractor who will be building the factory for me," Mr. Bello explained. "He's here to look over the site and scope out the local suppliers. Once we get past the protest meeting, we want to get started on the building right away."

After exchanging a few pleasantries about the weather with the two women, the gentlemen left to breakfast together. As soon as they had passed through the door, Margaret raised her eyebrows in Anne's direction.

"What a man!" she enthused, "If I weren't married I'd set my cap for him."

"Well, isn't he married?" Anne teased.

"No, my dear, he is not," Margaret told her. "He's been far too busy to get married. Right after college he went to the Middle East to supervise some building for a petroleum company. When he came back home a few years later he had enough money to start his own contracting business but his fiancée had gotten tired of waiting; so instead of starting his business in his own hometown, he moved to Middleborough to take advantage of Anthony Bello's business connections. They were in college together and they're as close as brothers. Jack's been running his own business for over five years now and he's very prosperous. Anthony's mom told us at club that Jack is a confirmed bachelor; but if I were young, pretty and single like you, I'd try to change that."

"Hmmnn," Anne said. "What makes you think I could catch him if I wanted to?"

Margaret snorted. "You really can't be that modest, Anne. Why just look at yourself!" She placed her hands lightly on Anne's shoulders and turned her toward the gilt-edged mirror hanging over the sideboard where the coffee and doughnuts were always at the ready.

Anne did not linger looking at her reflection. Instead she turned around immediately to give the older woman a quick little hug. "You do wonders for the morale," she said, "but I think you'd better find someone else to apply to be Mrs. Carter. I've just gotten here; I plan to live in Aunt Aggie's house. I have no intention of marrying anyone, much less someone who has headquarters in Middleborough."

Later that day, as was their daily lunchtime habit, Anne and Margaret walked the short distance down Elm Street, then across Main to Stella's cafe. Nearly all the town's various business people lunched at the cafe and it was always busy. Today, Anne and Margaret arrived a few minutes later than usual and found the room extremely crowded. Looking around for an available table, Anne saw Anthony Bello and Jack Carter seated in a booth near the rear. When Mr. Bello looked up and saw that she and Margaret were waiting for a table, he signaled for the two to join him and his companion.

The two gentlemen had already received menus and ice water and were apparently ready to place their orders as their menus were lying closed at their places. Stella soon bustled over with water and place settings for the new arrivals; and as Margaret and Anne generally refused menus and ordered only salads, she remained to take orders all around.

Stella soon fell into her usual easy banter with Jack Carter, who seemed quite taken with the friendly, if somewhat flashy, restaurant proprietress; and Anne felt some envy at the way the two, in typical American fashion, were able to swiftly fall into a familiar relationship; but her envy was not, she realized, based on any feelings she had for the newcomer. It was more that she belatedly realized how *wonderful it would be* if she would feel something for him.

She wished the newcomer could make her heart sing the way Matt did, for Jack Carter, a construction contractor, could build any house he wanted. If he were to care for her she would know it was for herself alone. Matt, on the other hand, wanted only to have an opportunity to acquire her house.

Anne was lost in thought when Stella returned with their orders, but she returned her attention to the friendly conversation at the table when her salad was placed in front of her just as Jack Carter made another teasing remark to Stella. Stella and Jack had a true gift for quickly developing warm relationships that Anne could only admire and could never hope to emulate. Perhaps it was because she was more British than American, but Anne's quiet reserve prevented her from engaging in light or flirtatious conversation.

When she and the others had nearly finished eating, Anne noticed Matt come into the cafe through a side door. She watched as Stella slung a casual arm across his shoulders and spoke to him in a voice too low to be heard across the crowded room. Matt laughed out loud at whatever little joke he had been told; and Anne felt a stab of vicious jealousy toward the woman who had evoked such a response; but even so, as Matt strode past the table, she pointedly looked away from him; and if he noticed her as he passed by, he gave no indication.

"I hope for your sake that Matt Stevens will not decide to join up with all those folks who are protesting the factory," Margaret commented to Anthony Bello as she watched the broad shoulders disappear into the small back room where he and Anne had lunched when she first arrived in Fairfield. "A lot of people would be convinced the factory was a bad thing if Matt was against it," she continued.

"I understand he has not yet said what his opinion is," Anne commented.

"Well, he won't be able to sit on the fence much longer," Margaret responded as she sought to locate her pocketbook. "At the meeting tomorrow night he'll have to swing one way or the other."

"Will you be at the meeting?" Anne asked.

"Oh, I wouldn't miss it!" Margaret exclaimed. "If Matt Stevens comes out on the right side of things, we'll see the wind knocked out of the sails of the protesters. It should be very interesting."

"I expect you are right," Anne commented as she pushed the rest of her salad away and began to gather her pocketbook and the notebook she always carried in case she needed to make note of something while at lunch.

Jack Carter signaled Stella for the check and insisted on treating the ladies, but he teased Stella about the ticket unmercifully and pretended to haggle with her about the price. Anne and Margaret left the restaurant together just as Jack Carter concluded the transaction by giving Stella a very large tip and simultaneously making a date with the lady for later the same evening; and although Stella treated his attentions as if they were her just due, Anne was sure that she saw something in the woman's eyes which indicated more than passing interest; and it also seemed to Anne that Stella told her good-bye in a friendlier way than usual, perhaps because she no longer thought of the beautiful younger woman as a rival now that a gentleman was seeming to pay total to attention to her while ignoring Anne's charm!

Anne's mind was only partly on Margaret's chatter as they took the short walk back to the office. "Why," she wondered, "did it seem there was a man for every woman in the world except herself? Margaret had her husband upon whom she doted, Mr. Bello had his adored 'Mama'; Janet and Bill were head over heels; and now Stella showed every sign of being totally smitten by Jack Carter. "Of course," she reminded herself wryly, "she could always have Rick." As far as she knew, that teenage boy had no interest whatever in acquiring her house. He, at least, wanted her for herself.

Anne smiled at the fanciful thought of giving consideration to the *unsuitably young* gentleman's infatuation. I guess I'm becoming Americanized already, she told herself, mentally taking herself to task for engaging in meaningless banter even though it had been only in a silent conversation within her own head.

The following evening, in spite of oppressive heat, the protest meeting attracted a large number of townspeople. The row of double doors at the entrance to the gymnasium had been left wide open; and two huge, industrial-size fans were positioned at the rear doors in an attempt to circulate the air in the stifling room. Anne was stationed near the entrance, offering packets to the citizens as they thronged into the room. Each packet contained a printed picture of the architect's conception of the planned factory building, a greeting from Anthony Bello to the community, a page containing the most frequent concerns Anne had uncovered in her telephone survey—along with Mr. Bello's responses to those concerns—and two employment applications, one for construction workers and the other for those who might wish to apply for positions in the factory when the time came for it to open.

Stapled together, the half dozen pages made pamphlets stiff enough to be usefully employed against the merciless warmth in the room. Throughout the huge old room the makeshift fans were swishing and fluttering, providing a rustling background for hundreds of conversations. Anne smiled as she greeted each newcomer and offered the packet, wondering if any of the papers would actually be read, or if perhaps Mr. Bello would have been better off distributing hundreds of paper fans rather than the carefully prepared material.

As the appointed moment for beginning approached, the stream of newcomers began to dwindle and Anne was able to look around at the crowd. At the far end of the room, on a stage situated beyond a hanging basketball goal, she saw men fiddling with the sound system. Off to one side of the stage, Matt Stevens was standing, in relaxed pose, wearing a light-colored jacket which seemed at home across his broad shoulders. He was engaged in conversation with a gentleman who, Anne had learned during the past week, was at the head of the protest movement.

"It must be true," Anne thought. "Matt must be taking sides against the factory." But a moment later she saw Matt engaged in conversation with Mr. Bello while his previous companion pointedly turned his back.

Anne distributed a few more of her packets and then turned toward the stage again. At that moment Matt turned full face toward her. He had not called her again and she had not seen him throughout the week; but now as she looked at him across the vastness of the room, the distance between them seemed to close as if she were drawing him into focus through a telescope. He probably doesn't even see me, she chided herself, as Matt turned away from her gaze and walked toward the podium set up at the middle of the stage. At this sign of the meeting beginning, she pulled out the folding chair which had been provided for her use and sat down to give her attention to the proceedings.

Matt began with a short welcoming speech, stating succinctly the purpose of the meeting. "As you know," he began, "Recently our local planning commission approved rezoning for a certain area on the north side of Fairfield. The area, only a couple of blocks in size, has been rezoned from single family residential to light industrial purposes. Some members of the community have protested this recent action. They have indicated that they feel the changes were made without full disclosure to the public and that these changes are contrary to the best interests of the citizens of Fairfield. This matter could end in a lawsuit." Matt looked around the assemblage slowly before beginning again.

"I am pleased, Ladies and Gentlemen, to be here tonight to lead the discussion of this matter. It is my hope that before the evening is over our community will have achieved unity and such a law suit can be avoided.

"It's extremely hot in this building, so at this time I would like to present to you Mr. Anthony Bello, who will tell you of the plans he has for bringing his factory here to Fairfield. After his presentation, we will hear prepared comments from the opposition, after which the meeting will be open for discussion.

"Mr. Bello," he said as he stepped aside.

There was applause from one side of the gymnasium, while from the other side came only a small smattering of hand claps. Anne realized that the gymnasium was split, as if for a sports contest, with all those for the factory seated primarily on the east side and those against on the west. In the front of the east side she noticed Mr. and Mrs. Bello proudly supporting their son, with Jack Carter and Stella seated close beside them. Meanwhile, Matt Stevens had seemed to take no side. At least, however, he was conducting the meeting in a fair fashion!

Mr. Bello asked for the lights to be dimmed; and on a large screen, a color picture flashed, showing the same artist's rendition which appeared on the pages of the pamphlets Anne had handed out. His speech was accompanied with the charts and other information Anne had spent the past week preparing and was clear and informative.

When he took his seat, Matt introduced the representative of the protest group. In contrast to Mr. Bello's carefully prepared remarks, this man's presentation was disjointed, high on opinion and short on fact. Never-the-less each of his increasingly shrill and opinionated remarks was met with a great deal of approval from the opposition side of the gymnasium.

When at last he finished, Matt returned to the podium. There was a murmur of expectation from the protest group. From the west side of the gymnasium a voice was heard to call out, "Give it to 'em, Matt!"

"It's hot here tonight folks and you've all been very patient. I hope we can wind this meeting up real soon. Please walk forward to the stage area if you have any inquiries you want to direct to either side. There is a microphone located just below me here and we would appreciate your using it, so we can all hear."

Half a dozen people quickly lined up on the west side, while only one came forward on the east. The one person who had come forward on the east wished only to support the zoning action and the new factory. After thanking him for the support, Mr. Bello patiently answered the questions of the protesters—questions which soon became repetitive.

Matt came forward again. "It seems to me that most of our major questions have been answered tonight," he said dismissing the general murmur of protest from half the gym area with a wave of his hand. "Now I would like a turn to speak.

"As a boy I lived in the area affected by this new zoning law. Today my daughter and I live only a few blocks away. The area has always been residential, and many believe it should remain so. Many people have looked to me to lead the opposition against bringing the new factory to Fairfield.

"A few weeks ago a group of residents from the north side neighborhood where I grew up came to my office to see me. They asked me to file a lawsuit against implementing the new zoning law. I took the matter under consideration but did not agree at that time to represent the group. When I heard that this meeting was being planned, I asked the protesters not to take formal action to file a suit until after this meeting to see if the disagreement could be settled amicably; but as I said, I did not agree to represent the protest group," he paused momentarily before continuing, "and I now publicly state that *I will not do so.* I believe this factory will be a very positive thing for Fairfield. I would like to be the first to welcome Anthony Bello to Fairfield."

"If however, any of you still wish to proceed with action to revoke the new zoning, please remain seated after this meeting has closed. I will give you a list of several attorneys who specialize in these cases and you can choose whomever you want to represent you, but as I stated, I personally will not do so.

"And now," he said, "those of you who would like to see a positive change come to Fairfield, stand up and leave. Protesters remain seated." With that Matt left the podium and walked across the stage and shook Anthony Bello's hand. He then walked briskly off stage and around the perimeter of the gym floor. All eyes were on him as he paused by Anne's little table and turned back toward the room.

The surprised assemblage began to talk among themselves as most of them rose to leave the building. Matt stood by the door shaking hands. It soon became apparent that the fifty or so persons who remained seated were in the vast minority. As the majority faction left the building, many looked with interest to determine who was still seated in the bleachers.

Under the curious eyes of the onlookers, several in the protest group began to rise and slip into the group that was thronging out of the building. As the protesters dwindled, they became more and more conspicuous. Finally, after some murmuring among themselves, a large group of them stood together and began to leave the room. The half dozen protesters who remained, finding all eyes upon them, looked back and forth among themselves; and then, finally, with shrugs of their shoulders, rose and left the building. Anne thought she heard Matt sigh when he looked again toward the bleachers and found all the seats now empty.

When all the citizens had at last filed out of the gym, Anne began to stack up her remaining pamphlets and to fold up the table and chair she had been using. Meanwhile, Matt and Anthony Bello were conversing a few feet from her.

"Hopefully, there won't be any more trouble now, Tony." Matt said. "Of course, you never know; I succeeded in embarrassing them tonight but they could still go out and hire another attorney tomorrow. I don't think they have a case at all, but it would be much more pleasant if they would just accept the situation. Your factory will be a great asset to this town and I don't understand why some folks can't see it."

"I don't mind saying, I'm glad this is over," Anthony said "I didn't know which way you were going; but I knew whichever way it was, you'd be taking most of the town with you."

"I don't think my opinion is quite that influential," Matt said, and then catching Anne's eye he continued, "Some folks don't value my opinions at all."

"Other people sometimes have *their own* opinions," Anne told him.

"Just leave those things here, Anne." Anthony told her, seeming only then to take note of her presence. "I borrowed them from the principal's office and the janitor will take them back tomorrow. By the way, the work you've done for me made my presentation a great deal easier. You have wonderful organizational skills and you have a full time job with me starting tomorrow morning if you want it. With this meeting behind me, I'm ready to get right to work on about ten thousand other details."

"Of course, I want to work for you," Anne replied coolly, even though she was both surprised and relieved to have so easily acquired a permanent position. "I'll see you in the morning."

"Do you need a ride home, Anne?" Matt asked her.

"Oh no, it's a wonderful night out. I'll walk."

"No you won't." Matt said firmly, putting his hand on her elbow and steering her out the door into the slightly cooler evening air where a number of people still stood in little knots conversing.

"Nice job, Matt," or "Congratulations!" several people called to him as he passed by with Anne's arm firmly in his grip; so Anne was relieved when they reached the shadows of the parking lot away from the eyes of the community.

"Really, Matt, I can walk; there's no need for you to go out of your way."

"So it's Matt again is it?" he crowed at her; and even in the shadows, he could see the color rise in her cheeks until they nearly matched the fiery color of her hair.

"I mean, Mr. Stevens," she stammered.

"Nonsense. Call me Matt, and you're not going to walk." He steered her to his car, maneuvered her inside, and had the car out of the lot and heading away from town before she could catch her breath.

# CHAPTER 22

"This is not the way home, Mr. Stevens" Anne told him frostily as soon as she had regained enough composure to speak.

"Ah, come on now, call me Matt," he coaxed.

"Mr. Stevens, I must get home; Janet will be wondering where I am."

"I doubt that. I happen to know your friend Bill Rodgers is keeping her busy almost all of the time." He did not mention how pleased he had recently been to hear of Rodgers' involvement with the newcomer, having feared that young gentleman might have formed a relationship with Anne which was stronger than a usual friendship.

"Janet *and* Bill will wonder where I am," she said stubbornly.

"Anne, I won't keep you out too long," Matt told her, his bantering tone suddenly gone, "But I really want to talk to you for a few minutes. Something has happened between us that I don't like and I don't understand. I thought you might grow to care for me; but now it seems you can hardly stand me. Why, Anne?"

"Perhaps I figured out that you weren't interested in me at all. It's my house you want. For some reason you've got an obsession about it. Even Aunt Aggie said you'd give the moon for it. You weren't able to get it from her, but you thought you'd have an easy time getting it from me. Your so-called friendship was just a way to keep your hand in the pie until I gave up and sold it to you."

"Is that what you think, Anne?"

"It's the truth, isn't it?"

"No, Anne, it's not the truth at all. Believe me, I no longer wish to buy your house."

"If you didn't want to buy my house why did you make the *generous* offer Mr. Thomas conveyed to me? And if you weren't trying to pull the wool over my eyes, why did you make the offer *anonymously?*"

By this time Matt had driven the car to the same general area of the countryside where Anne had recently gone with Bill and Janet several times for driving lessons. The roads were completely deserted at this hour this far out in the country.

Matt drove for a few more minutes, saying nothing. When he reached a Y crossing in the road, he pulled onto the short-clipped grass between the two branching roads and stopped the car. He turned to Anne with naked love and compassion on his face.

"Anne, Sweetheart..."

"I'm not your sweetheart!"

"Well, I want you to be."

"What!"

"Anne, I'm in love with you; can't you tell?"

"You're in love with my house, that's all."

"It was a mistake to try to buy your house; at least it was a mistake after you came here to live. I'm really sorry; please forgive me." He had moved closer to her and now he encircled her shoulders with his arm and lightly caressed her upper arm. "Please give me a chance, Anne." His voice was almost a whisper.

Anne was deeply aware of his hand on her shoulder, of his eyes which had captured hers and held them so tightly that she could not look away, of his lips which second by second seemed to grow closer to her own and more desirable. She was desperately torn between her surging feelings for this man and the reality of the situation *as she saw* it. Frustration at her confusion rose to her throat and caught there in a tiny sob.

The sound of the little sob completely ended Matt's composure. He pulled her close to him, seeking her hair and

130

entwining his strong slender fingers within its silken fragrance, pulling her toward him until she could feel the slight stubble of his beard against her cheek. "Poor baby, poor baby," he murmured. "It must have been so difficult for you to come here all alone with Aggie gone. I want to hold you sweetheart; I want to love you; I want to take care of you."

The sound of his voice, low in her ear, whispering endearments, was mesmerizing to Anne. She pulled away slightly, letting her head droop forward so that Matt could not see her eyes while she fought her confusion.

He held her loosely for a moment, his lips resting against her hair just above her forehead, then with a groan he pulled her toward him once more and took her quivering lips against his own, which were firm and demanding.

Moments passed as he kissed Anne, invading her mouth, invading her soul, taking her into his possession. Anne was floating far away; she was on a cloud and there was nobody else there but herself and Matt. She could not resist him. She was his.

Eventually, of course, Matt was forced to pull away from the kiss in order to breathe and to release the pressure of having remained too long in one position. He shifted her body a little to draw nearer to her and she was surprised and slightly frightened by his intensity as he held her. But the fright was far overridden by the need to be closer to him; she wanted to blend herself into him, wanted to become one with him. The urge to allow herself to be drawn into his very being was a completely unfamiliar experience for her. She had never responded to a man this way before.

He kissed her neck, then rained warm kisses all the way back around to her mouth. His hand stroked her hair away from her face and he gazed at her eyes with such intensity that she began to shake.

It was at that moment that a car came along on one of the roads of the forking Y. Anne pulled away from Matt as the car turned onto the adjoining road, turning her head so her face would not be visible in the lights of the car as it swung back along the other road of the Y.

Matt realized at once that the magic had been lost, but he did not relinquish his hold on her. Though he held her more loosely he left his arms around her and sought once more to capture her eyes with his own.

"Anne," he said, "It's not your house I want. It's you. Will you marry me?"

"Marry you?" Anne came crashing back to reality. "You really would do anything to get my house, wouldn't you?"

"Anne, you can't think that. Of course I wouldn't marry you just to get a house! I told you I don't want your house." But Anne's senses had returned the moment he said the word *house,* or at least she thought they had. Matt had tried to buy the house from her and he had tried again to buy it through Mr. Thomas. It wasn't one bit stranger to think he'd marry her for the house than to think he'd marry her for herself, for after all he hardly knew her.

Still, there was a deep dull ache in Anne's heart and a yearning in her very soul to once again press herself into Matt's arms and abandon herself to the bliss of his embrace; but she forced herself to resist her weakness for him.

"Take me home," she said dully.

"Anne, please..."

"Take me home."

Reluctantly Matt turned on the engine and pulled back onto the road to take Anne home, though he vowed silently to himself that somehow he would overcome her stubborn conviction that he wanted her house. He had wanted the house...once. Now, though, there was no house in the world he could desire more than he desired to possess this fiery, auburn-haired vixen who spoke in a clipped accent that could cut a man in two.

"Anne, about Mr. Thomas..."

"Don't try to deny it. I *know* you're the one who made the offer."

"Have it your way then, Anne. We won't talk about it anymore," Matt said grimly. He had been about to tell her that he had withdrawn his offer, for not only did he no longer want to buy the house from her, he now wanted to help her keep it. Truthfully he wanted to give her anything she wanted, but darn it, she was off the wall on this house business. He would *not* give up, but for now he would let the matter ride.

"Good-bye, Mr. Stevens," Anne said, as he pulled to a stop in her circular drive; and then, as Matt leaned over to switch off the ignition, she continued icily, "Don't bother getting out; I'll be fine."

"*Goodnight* then, Anne," he said gently.

Anne slid out of the car and shut the door with only a little more force than necessary. As she forced her trembling fingers to insert her key in the lock, she heard Matt's tires crunching against the gravel in the driveway as he slowly pulled away. Tears were already starting in her eyes.

# CHAPTER 23

Because Anne had been obliged to attend the meeting, Bill had taken Janet into the city to see a movie. Now Anne was glad they were not at home as she was in no mood for conversation. She scribbled a note to tell her friends she was tired and had gone to bed; then she wearily climbed the gracefully curved staircase to the lovely old-fashioned room which contained everything which was home to her.

There in the room prepared for her by the one person in the world who had loved her unconditionally, she allowed herself the luxury of letting a few of her welling tears squeeze out from beneath the delicate lashes that covered her now sad green eyes. They were tears of humiliation as well as regret, humiliation that she had so easily responded to Matt's lovemaking and regret that, on his part at least, the lovemaking had been merely a sham designed to render her helpless in his arms so he could get his hands on her house.

She burned alternately with shame and longing as her thoughts returned inexorably to the moments in Matt's car when he had caressed her, sweet-talked her, and nearly broken her resistance with the tenderness he had feigned.

Mechanically she took off her dress and opened her closet for a hanger, planning to hang the dress near an open window to air overnight. Although it had been hot in the gymnasium, she had been in a breeze most of the time; and to spare a cleaning bill, she thought the dress could probably be worn another time.

As she searched in the dim light of the closet for an empty hanger, her eyes fell on the lovely russet pant suit Matt had purchased for her. It was still far too warm to wear the garment; but she had tried it on soon after it was purchased and had found that it did call forth the bright lights in her hair as Matt had predicted.

Without doubt it was one of the most attractive casual outfits she had ever owned, and she longed to wear it. Just now, however, the sight of the garment was more than she could stand. She reached out and clenched a handful of its soft fabric in one hand and, incongruously, gently stroked it with the other hand, her mixed feelings about Matt Stevens evidently being transferred to the wearing apparel. When she suddenly realized that she was standing in the closet transfixed by the garment, she slammed the closet door shut and yanked her dress off over her shoulders, uncharacteristically tossing it across a chair in the corner of her room, after which she kicked her shoes in the same general direction before throwing herself across the bed for a good cry.

Not surprisingly, Anne did not soon fall asleep; and thus as the clock slowly moved forward into the wee morning hours, she became increasingly worried about Bill and Janet, who had not yet returned. She had nearly decided to phone the police to inquire about a possible accident when at last she heard them pull into the drive.

A few moments later when Janet bounded up the staircase, taking the stairs two by two, she found Anne tightening the sash on her robe.

"I'm sorry, Anne. Did I wake you?"

"No, I haven't been asleep."

Janet detected something slightly wrong with her friend's tone of voice. "Oh," she said carefully, "Is something wrong?"

"Not really," Anne said; and then, attempting to sound positive, she said, as cheerfully as possible, "Mr. Bello gave me a full time job."

"That's wonderful, but..."

"But what?"

"That's what I want to know. Why are you unhappy?"

"Just a thing with Matt Stevens. He brought me home."

"You ought to give him a chance, Anne."

"If he was serious, I would," Anne replied. "Now let's change the subject. You are very late." She wagged her finger at her friend.

"I have a good reason to be late."

"What is your reason, if I might ask?"

"This!" Janet showed her finger on which glinted a tiny diamond in a shiny gold circlet. "I'm engaged. Bill told me he knew it was a little soon to be asking, but he didn't want me going back to England, so he had to work fast."

"Oh Janet, how wonderful! You'll be staying here."

"If you have no objections, we'd like to live in the apartment. It's almost done and that's a good thing. Bill wants to be married before his fall classes start so we can get away for a short trip. We're only going to wait to be married until Mums and Dad can arrange to come here. I want them to be at the wedding."

"Of course you can stay in the apartment. It's what Aunt Aggie would have wanted," Anne hugged her friend.

The two sat up another hour as Janet talked about life and fate and how wonderful it was that Anne had come to the States and that she had come to see her and thus met Bill. As her friend prattled on and on, Anne tried not to feel jealous, but it was difficult not to think of how wonderful it would be if she too could find true love—someone who made her heart soar the way Matt Stevens did and whose feelings for her were as strong as hers for him.

At last Janet arose from where she had perched herself on Anne's bed and exclaimed at the hour showing on the clock. "Oh dear, look at the time. You have to be at work in a few hours!" After one more hug she bustled out of the room leaving Anne alone with her thoughts.

Sometime in the next hour or so, Anne at last managed to fall asleep. It seemed like only moments later when her alarm clock began to buzz and she was forced to get up to go to work.

In spite of near total exhaustion, she slipped out the side door of the house at the same hour as always and began the walk toward town in the cool morning air. She was as impeccably dressed as ever, but a close observer may have noticed pale purplish circles in the delicate skin beneath her green eyes.

Arriving at the office a few minutes before nine o'clock, she spent the first half hour cleaning her desk of the residue left from the flurry of preparations for the previous evening's meeting. Margaret directed several incoming calls to her office from various business associates who had messages for Mr. Bello and Anne handled everything with her usual calm efficiency. The rhythm of her work was soothing and she began to feel more herself as the minutes sped by.

At about 9:45 Mr. Bello phoned and explained that he was hung up at a Chamber of Commerce breakfast meeting. She jotted down some instructions and gave him a couple of messages she thought might be important before returning to the task at hand, writing a 'thank you' note to place in the local newspaper to thank the community for the spirit of cooperation which had prevailed at the meeting. As soon as she had an opportunity, she would ask Mr. Bello what he thought of running the ad.

At mid-morning she went into the front office to share a cup of coffee and a cookie with Margaret. She had skipped breakfast again and was grateful for Margaret's hospitality.

Before she had returned to her own office, Mr. Thomas came in and greeted her with a big smile. "There was quite a conversation about Mr. Stevens this morning at the Chamber meeting," he said jovially. "He did a good thing for this community last night; and by the way, Mr. Bello told me that he gave you a ride after the meeting. I hope that means you two have settled your differences."

"What differences do you mean?" Anne asked.

"Well... uh...you know what I mean," Mr. Thomas said. Apparently feeling he had spoken out of turn, he now seemed to be at a loss for words.

"You mean Matt made the anonymous offer to buy my house, don't you?" Anne asked him bluntly.

"Now, Anne, he was just trying to help you out," Mr. Thomas told her lamely, nervously pushing his thin hair back from his forehead. "I don't think he planned on having you be upset by it."

"The man is impossible!" Anne exclaimed. "I have to tell him I don't want to sell the house every time I run into him. I hope you told him what I thought of his offer."

"Oh, I told him all right, Anne; but that was before he..." He seemed to think better about continuing the train of thought. With a wave of his hand he passed on toward his own office and uncharacteristically closed the door behind him, leaving Anne to make small talk with Margaret while she fought down a feeling of annoyance that her peace of mind had been shattered once more by a conversation about *Matt Stevens* and *selling her house!*

Anne soon returned to her office and with her usual efficiency had completed all the work Mr. Bello had requested in his phone conversation by the time he arrived an hour later.

"Did you have a good time with Matt Stevens last night?" he asked Anne.

"Really," Anne replied, exasperated, "He just took me home!"

Anthony Bello looked at her in surprise. He had never seen Anne get ruffled before. Probably a lover's tiff, he thought, for he had heard a rumor from Mr. Thomas only that morning that Matt Stevens was sweet on the beautiful English girl. He thought the girl looked tired. Probably she had stayed up too late last night with that young man.

"I've made a list of a few more things here, Anne." he said pleasantly. "Wait until after lunch to begin and leave as soon as you're finished. You've worked hard ever since I hired you. I don't want to wear you out."

"Thank you, Mr. Bello," Anne said, already sorry for the sharp tone of her earlier outburst. "I could use some rest."

Then quickly, before he had to leave the office once again she asked him to look at the 'thank you' ad she had prepared.

"What a great idea, Anne," he said when she had shown him the draft. "I'll drop this off at the newspaper office on my way over to the factory site. I think when we get the factory started I'll put you in charge of PR."

As he left the office, Anne began to mentally organize the few tasks remaining for the day. She was pleased at Mr. Bello's reaction to the project she had undertaken on her own initiative. Maybe he wasn't really serious about the PR job, but at least he appreciated her work. Appreciation was something she had never experienced while employed at the firm of Garold and Garold.

That afternoon, Anne finished her work quickly and walked home through the sleepy little town, loathe to phone Bill to ask him to come for her. When she arrived home, she found the house empty and went to her room for a long nap; then, somewhat refreshed, she began to make notes of possible ideas for Janet's wedding. She spent the evening discussing those plans with Janet and Bill even though her own sorrows continued to dwell in the dark corners of her mind.

Finally, there came a moment when Bill caught her staring off into space. "Knock, knock," he said in order to regain her attention. "A penny for your thoughts."

"They aren't worth it," Anne answered. "I was just thinking about Matt Stevens making an offer for this house. I wonder why he wants it so much. Margaret told me he lives in a perfectly charming little house already."

"Well, Anne, he didn't have that house yet the first time he tried to buy this one. I don't know exactly why he wants this one so much except it's one of the nicest in town. I do know I was annoyed the first time he approached Aggie because I knew her a whole lot better than he did. I knew what the house meant to her; and I was afraid if he talked her into selling, she'd grieve herself to death about it. Of course, if she had sold, it would have messed up my plans about the apartment; so I couldn't say anything without seeming selfish."

"Nobody would ever think you're selfish!" Janet exclaimed.

"I think she likes me," Bill said with a wry grin at Anne as he gave Janet a playful punch in the shoulder.

"Anyway, I was wrong about Matt."

"In what way were you wrong?" Anne asked.

"For a while I thought he was up to something about the estate. I heard that after Aggie died he decided he still wanted to buy the house. I thought he might be abusing his position as administrator and planning to pick it up for a lot less than it's worth. Then a couple of days ago I ran into your friend Margaret from Thomas's office and made the mistake of implying that to her. She set me straight in no uncertain terms." He seemed to shudder at the memory. "She told me that the price Stevens offered for the house was outrageous all right—outrageously high! I guess I just had my back up." he concluded. "I shouldn't have jumped to conclusions."

"I thought you acted a little strange about Matt the first day I arrived here!" Anne exclaimed.

"At that time I thought he was out to fleece you," Bill admitted. "And I'd also heard he was against the new factory coming in. It turned out I was wrong about that, too."

"We all make mistakes," Anne told him thoughtfully.

The following morning she was back at work, bright and early as usual and unaccountably feeling more like her usual self. Margaret detected her brighter spirits immediately and incorrectly assumed that Anne had been cheered by improved relations with

Matt Stevens. "Did you hear from Matt Stevens last night?" she asked mischievously.

"No." Anne replied shortly, her mood suddenly cooler. "Is there some reason I should have?"

"Well, now, Honey, it's no secret around here how he feels about you," Margaret admonished her. "He wanted to buy that house to help you out; and when that idea upset you, he hightailed it right back in here to cancel his offer. It's pretty obvious you're more than just a client to him."

Anne stared at her trying to absorb what she'd said. "He canceled the offer?"

"Well, yes, he did. Didn't Mr. Thomas tell you?"

"He didn't mention it," Anne said as her thoughts raced away with the new information. *Matt canceled his offer.* Had he really changed his mind or did he have some other plan for getting the house he thought would work better? Like sweet-talking her, for instance. One thing was true about Margaret's comments, however. She *was* more than a client to him, of that she was sure. She was a *challenge.*

# CHAPTER 24

Mr. Bello was off and running with factory business at work and Janet was off and running with wedding plans at home, so Anne had very little time for thinking about herself during the next few days.

On Saturday morning, when Janet and Bill had gone to the city to make some of their wedding arrangements, she settled herself at Aunt Aggie's desk, trying to focus her mind on the 'to do' list for Janet's wedding; but in spite of her determination to resist his blandishments, she found herself missing Matt Stevens and thinking back over all that had transpired between them since her arrival in the United States. When her eyes spotted the small, never-opened envelope Mr. Thomas had given her weeks before containing the offer for her house, she reached for it almost without thinking. Using Aunt Aggie's small ivory letter opener, she carefully slit the envelope. The figure she encountered was certainly generous—it was more than generous she realized as she mentally converted the dollar figure into pounds; and surely, as Mr. Thomas had said, more than the house was worth. *Why would Matt make such an offer? Was he out of his mind; would he really 'give the moon' for this house?*

With that thought in mind, she picked up Aunt Aggie's journal and opened it—as every time she opened it now—to the offending page. Starting once more at, "give the moon" she then resolutely turned the page. After all, just because Matt Stevens wanted to buy her house, she shouldn't deny herself the pleasure of reading Aunt Aggie's journal. It was the only way she could feel close to her now.

Anne read one page, then another, swiftly turning pages as her eyes hungrily ate up the words.

Aunt Aggie had an interesting writing style, telling little jokes on herself here and there; but there were few real events recorded. She told of the weather, the few visitors who had called, occasional club meetings she had attended and even jotted down a recipe she wanted to try. Anne turned another page and saw splotches in the ink. "Could Aunt Aggie have been crying?"

The name STEVENS leaped from the page. Anne read the entry, unconsciously setting her mouth in a hard firm line as she skimmed the words, trying to determine what Stevens might have done to upset her aunt.

"That nice young Mr. Stevens came to see me again today. I'm sure he came to renew his offer to buy the house, but he didn't say a word about it. The inner door was open and when he came up to the screen door he could see me sitting at the table bawling like a baby. I still am, although he did his best to cheer me up. Poor old Mabel Baker is dying. She's been my best friend ever since I first came to Fairfield. Her daughter called me today. BREAST CANCER— already quite advanced. The dear, silly old fool. She must have known about it for a long time and just let it go. Now it's too late. No chance at all. How will I live without her?"

The next day the entry said: "Matt Stevens was back again today. Said he was taking me to lunch. He wasn't going to just sit back and let me cry all day again. Lunch was delicious and he didn't say a word about the house. Asked if he could come again and bring his daughter. I don't know why he wants to bother with an old woman but he's welcome to come whenever he wants. He seems lonely. Maybe he needs a friend, too."

Many more entries in the journal mentioned Matt's name: *"He's becoming like a son to me,"* and a few days later *"I don't know how I would have gotten through Mabel's funeral without Matt Stevens."*

A week later Aggie recorded that she had asked Matt outright if he was hanging around trying to sweeten her up so she'd sell him the house. She had underlined an entry:

*"He has bought another house.* Says he wouldn't hear of me giving up this one. He's *happy right where he is."*

The crisis about Mabel having sadly resolved itself, there were fewer entries about Matt for a while, but after a dozen pages Anne read: "I have asked Matt to come over when he has time—it's a good thing to have a lawyer for a friend. He comes to me; I don't have to go out. I'm going to ask him to accept power of attorney over me in the event that I become unable to make my own decisions. Mabel's death has reminded me that I won't live forever. I do wish Anne would come stay with me soon. I want her here while I'm still able to get out and about and show her the sights and enjoy her company, and lately I've been thinking…"

Almost at the end of the book now, Anne had tears in her eyes as she read about the last days before her aunt passed away. Such a flurry of preparations going on; so much happiness in anticipation of *her* arrival. If only she had come sooner!

She had nearly reached the last of the entries when she read: "I know I'm superstitious but I have not breathed a word about Anne's arrival to Matt. I don't believe I've even mentioned that I HAVE a niece. I have told him that I will have a surprise for him in a couple of weeks, but I haven't said what it will be. When Anne comes, I will have some of that applesauce cake he loves — ostensibly that will be the surprise, but the real surprise will be Anne. I have a feeling about those two. Telling him about her would jinx it for sure, but when he sees her...

"Can it really happen? Could this old house one day be filled with children as I've always wanted—starting with that sweet little Karen? She's like a dear little granddaughter already. Oh how I pray my dream will come true."

The entries that followed were just countdowns. "Two weeks now until Anne comes, ten more days..."

The rest of the pages were blank. Anne found herself stroking the first blank page. On the facing page Aunt Aggie's words made her seem vibrant, alive, very much of the here and now. On the next page she was gone. Two pages, one with so much joy and hope, the other just empty—it was like viewing the passing of Aggie's soul.

Anne began to cry. First she cried for the loss of her aunt, the tears flowing just as swiftly as they had the first day when she received news of her loss when she was still in London. Next she cried from shame. She had held Matt Stevens in contempt, believed his friendship—no his romance with her—was a ruse designed to acquire this silly house, but she hadn't really known him as Aunt Aggie did. Aunt Aggie had trusted him with her power of attorney to make decisions for her in the event she had become helpless. Why Aunt Aggie would even have given Anne herself to Matt with complete trust that belonging to him would be a wonderful thing!

Aunt Aggie was a wise woman. The conclusion Anne reached was inescapable. She had made a mistake. She had misjudged Matt Stevens and treated him badly—treated badly the one man she had ever fallen in love with—yes fallen in love with! All the time she had tried to ignore that fact, to hide from it, to run from it, it had been there. She loved Matt Stevens. And she didn't want to lose him. Anne jumped up and ran from the house. Bill would just have to take her to town right now!

But Bill isn't here, she reminded herself in dismay as her feet hit the graveled drive. When a solution occurred to her, she didn't think twice. Even though her lessons in driving had not yet progressed to the point of practice on populated streets, she jumped into the driver's seat of Aunt Aggie's car.

A few tense minutes later she found herself on Fairfield's main street where a surprising number of vehicles had converged on the town square for Saturday morning business. There was only one parking place available on the street, a single space, actually quite generously sized; but Anne knew she would never maneuver the car into it without mishap. She slowly turned the car into the bank's parking lot, edging it in, foot by foot, then inch by inch in her fear she would hit the building. Once the car was parked she ran across the lot and, scarcely stopping to look for traffic, ran across the road and into Matt's office.

Inside she found the outer desk occupied by Matt's secretary who looked up in surprise as Anne rushed in the door.

"Can I help you?" the secretary asked coolly.

"Is Matt...I mean Mr. Stevens in?" Anne asked.

"He's with a client right now," she was told in a frosty tone. Only then did Anne realize that, so anxious had she been to get to Matt, she had run out in frayed old shorts and a faded blouse which had once belonged to Aunt Aggie and was tight across the bosom. No make-up either. She must look a fright. What would Matt think?

"I'll...come back...later," Anne stammered and retreated through the still-open door, as happy now to make her escape as she had been a moment earlier to burst through the door.

She trudged down the street toward home, her embarrassment having caused her to temporarily forget she had brought the car. When a block later she remembered it, she decided she'd have Bill and Janet bring it home later. She shouldn't be driving anyway as she still did not have her license.

A few minutes later, Anne arrived back at her house and let herself in the door she had left unlocked in her haste to leave. She was barely inside the door when a car careened into the drive. She looked out and saw Matt bounding from the seat of his small sports car.

"Anne, Anne!" he called as he ran across the few feet to the door and began to pound on the frame surrounding the screen. "Are you here?"

"What is it?" she asked, frightened into thinking he might bear bad news.

"That's what I want to know," he demanded. "My secretary said you came down there and burst through the door looking like something the cats dragged in. She thought something must be wrong with you."

By now Matt had his hands on her upper arms and was holding her away from him, searching her for any signs of the problem that

146

had sent her rushing to his door. To his surprise she began to chuckle and was soon almost overcome with the giggles.

"What's so darn funny?" he asked.

"Oh Matt," Anne said to him, realizing at last the depth of his caring. "I was so wrong about you."

"Of course you were wrong about me, but I don't think it's all that funny."

At that Anne laughed harder than ever.

"Well at least you seem to have a sense of humor," Matt commented dryly, "And besides," he said, surveying her, "You're about the cutest thing I ever saw the cats drag in."

Before anymore could be said, Anne took him by the hand and let him into the little sitting room where she pulled him down onto the settee beside her. Without any further preliminaries, she blurted. "If you'll still have me, I will marry you."

"You will what!"

"Marry you."

"Did I ask you to marry me?"

"Of course you did," she replied, a slight alarm building in her chest.

"You're right, I did," Matt said with a grin; and having regained his composure, he pulled the beautiful red-haired English beauty into his arms and kissed her for a long time. When he finally pulled his lips away, it was only to whisper, "Just tell me one thing; tell me I'm not dreaming."

"It's true," she told him softly. "I love you. I've always loved you. I was so confused. Let's never quarrel again." And she offered her lips to be kissed once more.

It was much later, when Matt was finally satisfied that he had indeed won her over, that she carefully asked him to explain his interest in the house.

# CHAPTER 25

"I promise you, Matt, I will never argue with you about this house again, but I hope you will answer one question for me before we put the issue aside forever;" Anne said in her careful, clearly-spoken, clipped English.

"I would have answered anything you asked, anytime you asked from the first time I met you," Matt replied. "I fell in love with you the moment I saw you sitting in that taxi bawling your eyes out, although I admit I fought it for a while," he chuckled as he nuzzled her cheek, reveling in her closeness.

"I only wonder why, after you had already purchased a house for you and Karen to live in, you still tried to buy this one after my aunt died."

"Oh, Sweetheart," he sighed. "My intentions were honorable. When Agatha died I couldn't bear the thought of strangers coming in to buy the house at the highest bid. She loved the place so much it would have seemed like I was betraying her friendship if I didn't do what I could to keep that from happening. I decided to live here myself and sell the other place, or rent it or whatever. I just wanted to be sure that this house was in good hands.

"I was in a kind of awkward position, being the administrator of the estate, so I had Thomas come in and appraise the place and then enter an offer for me at ten percent more than the appraisal." He turned slightly to look squarely into Anne's eyes. "I assure you the offer was more than fair. This whole area has been so depressed lately that it's likely there would have been no other decent offers for a house this large and expensive to maintain.

"After you came here to live I renewed my offer because I knew you didn't have enough money coming to you to afford it for very long. The situation was more than I could stand. This house, which I love, seemed doomed to eventually fall into someone's hands besides yours and I wanted that someone to be me. I went to see Thomas and nearly doubled my original offer because I wanted to do my best to get you off on the right foot here in Fairfield. From a business standpoint it was foolish; but, like I said, as soon as met you I was ready to do foolish things if I thought they would help you."

He paused for a moment before continuing. "And, Anne, I can afford it. My grandfather and my father both did very well in life. When Dad passed away he left me an enormous sum. I'm doing pretty well with my law practice, too. Every year I make a lot more than I can spend, and I have a good brokerage firm taking care of it all." He rubbed his chin against her bright auburn hair. "Now that we're getting married you can afford the house and you don't have to work unless you want to."

"You won't mind if I do, though!" Anne exclaimed with some consternation, thinking of how well she enjoyed her job and the feeling of independence it engendered.

"Of course not," Matt assured her. "I like both Annes—the cool sophisticated one who wears dress-up clothes to work and the one who wears shorts and tee shirts around the house."

Anne blushed at his reference to her wearing apparel and quickly asked another question, both to satisfy her curiosity and to cover her sudden self-consciousness. "I don't even understand why you were trying to buy the house in the first place when it wasn't listed for sale. Why, Matt?"

"When I first tried to buy the house, I wanted it very badly," he admitted as he pulled her closer to him, settling her beneath his arm with her head resting against his shoulder. "You'll understand why when I've told you more about my history—and the history of this house."

"Well then, tell me," she encouraged him.

"In the first place, did you know that in the beginning, when this house was built, there were two of them, identical in every way except this one was here on the south edge of town and the other one was on the north edge?"

"Really!" she said in surprise. "What happened to the other one?"

"It burned to the ground a few years ago. There's nothing but a field of high weeds where it used to be." He shook his head sadly before continuing. "Incidentally, if you wonder, it's the field where the new novelty plant is going to be built. Both houses were built in the late eighteen-hundreds for the twin daughters of a prominent Fairfield banker. The old guy wanted to be sure his daughters always had the best of everything, so he gave them the houses for wedding gifts. It's a local legend—they had a huge double wedding, then the four of them went abroad for a honeymoon. By the time they returned, the houses were complete. When the twins moved into the houses, it was supposedly the first time they had ever slept a night under different roofs.

"The house on the north end was owned by Martha Ann Campbell. She had a house full of children and a ne'er-do-well husband. She died young and the house had to be sold to pay her debts. It changed hands a few times and my grandfather ended up buying it many years later.

"My father was raised there and I grew up there until I was a teenager. When my mother died, my father was so disheartened he wouldn't even stay in town anymore. He sold the house and joined the Peace Corps for a few years. I was sent to a military school."

"How sad for you," Anne murmured, knowing that private schools were not usual in the United States as they were in England. Here, it seemed, people usually thought of such schools as places of punishment for difficult children.

"Actually, it was good for me," he replied with a shrug. "We lost Mom suddenly, and if it hadn't been for the discipline at the school I might have gone off the deep end for a while." He squeezed Anne against him.

"Anyway, when Dad came back he lived in a small apartment above the law office for the rest of his life. It was perfect for him—he never remarried; he was married to his practice.

"Meanwhile, I was busy going to college and law school. I married young and I didn't know my wife as well as I should have when we got married. I was full of vinegar and didn't want to wait."

"And then you lost her?" Anne asked sympathetically. "How ever did you get through it?"

"It was hard," he admitted. "I blamed myself. I knew Sarah had a drinking problem, but I didn't want to deal with it. I just kept working later and later because I didn't want to come home at night. I guess she felt more and more alone and drank more and more because of it. Then we found out she was pregnant.

"She pulled herself together and stayed sober the whole nine months of the pregnancy, but after Karen was born she started to slip again. She called me one night when I was working late and asked me to come home. I could hardly understand what she was saying.

"I told her bluntly that she was drunk and ordered her to put the housekeeper on the phone. I heard the phone drop and I was waiting impatiently for Mrs. Berry to come on the line. When she finally did, I told her to get Sarah undressed and put her to bed. Mrs. Berry told me Sarah had run out of the house leaving the door wide open and she had heard her car start. She had run to the phone to call me and discovered it dangling off the hook.

"I knew at that moment how it would end," he said flatly as Anne sympathetically stroked the back of the perfect hand which was draped across her shoulder. "I knew she would never come back alive.

"So you see, I was to blame," he concluded somberly. "I should have come home, not only that night, but all the other nights. I wasn't a very good husband." He sighed ruefully. "Maybe you

151

won't want to marry me after all now that you know how I behaved last time?"

"Oh, Matt," Anne said softly. "You did the best you could. Sometimes people have problems. I want to marry you more than anything in the world—you're the only man I want to marry and I know you'll be a wonderful husband; and God willing, I will be a good wife to you."

Matthew Stevens hugged his beautiful fiancée close against his heart and lowered his mouth against her soft curving lips. Only after another long and luxuriant kiss did he begin to speak again.

"Now" he said, "About this house. It was originally owned by Mary Ann Burton.

"Although her sister, Martha Ann, had half a dozen children, Mary Ann never had any children at all; and she lived to be an old, old woman. When she passed away, the house was left to all her sister's children and their descendants, but they were all as poor as church mice so this house was sold out of their family too. Your uncle bought it from the estate and he and your aunt lived here all their married life."

"But I still don't understand why you wanted to buy this house from Aunt Aggie," Anne said, struggling to see how all that he had told her fit together.

"At first after Sarah was killed, I stayed on in the house where we had lived. I kept the housekeeper on, but Sarah's mother and father helped with Karen's care and started to spend more and more time with her. He shook his head. "I wanted her to have a relationship with them, but after a while it seemed they were taking over and I was gradually losing her. Then Dad passed away and it seemed like a good time to move back to Fairfield and take over his practice. I thought Karen would be better off growing up here than in the city and it would give me a chance to reconnect with her. I couldn't very well live in Dad's apartment with a little girl to raise, although I did stay there for several months. I looked at every vacant house in town and none seemed right for us. Then one day I was driving down the river road and I happened to look over and see this house.

"Aggie was there in the back garden leaning on her hoe. The house where I was raised was gone, burned up—not a trace left. The idea struck me that if she would sell me *this* house, I could bring Karen here and raise her in a house which was *exactly* like the one I was raised in." Once more he gave a little rueful shake of his head. "I guess I wasn't thinking too clearly at the time.

"Anyway, after I came here a few times, I got friendly with Aggie. I started bringing Karen over and she loved your aunt and Agatha seemed to really enjoy spending time with her. In the end, although Aggie refused to sell me the house, she gave me something better— her friendship. One day at her suggestion, I showed Karen all through the house including the room which corresponded to the one I had as a boy. Walking through this house brought my mother back to me. I began to recall the joy of her life instead of simply the pain of her death; and in some strange way when I began to remember my mother again, I began to heal a little from the tragedy of Sarah's death too.

"And that, my dear," he smiled, "is the whole story except that—" he paused for maximum impact, "the last time I saw Aggie, just a few days before her death, she sat me down right here in this room for a little lecture. She told me she knew that before I bought my little house I had my heart set on owning this one. She said she was sorry she could never *sell* it to me because she thought of me almost like a son but she said, maybe someday, after she was gone, I'd have another chance to *acquire* it. She told me she hoped I'd never forget that this house was designed for love and laughter and that she hoped someday it would finally have some children living in it, and then (another pause) she told me to be sure and come see her the following week. She said she was planning a wonderful surprise for me."

"What do you think the surprise was going to be?" Anne asked him, speaking very slowly.

"I think maybe *our Aunt Aggie* was planning a little matchmaking," he answered, "What do you think?"

"I think you're right," Anne told him and then, quite brazenly, she pulled his head toward her as she raised her lips toward him. "I think we should have the wedding right here at the house," she whispered just before their lips met.

"I wouldn't have it any other way," he said softly before lowering his head the last quarter inch for his lips to meet those of his beloved.

# EPILOGUE

A few weeks later, Aunt Aggie's secret hope was fulfilled when a wedding took place between her lovely niece and the man who had been as dear to Aggie as if he was her own son. Anne was comforted by knowing that even though Aunt Aggie could not be present at the wedding her blessing had been given to the union.

The wedding was held in Aunt Aggie's backyard garden and the occasion was made more joyous by something which Aunt Aggie could not have foreseen. It was a double wedding ceremony which took place on a warm August day with late summer flowers for a backdrop. It featured two British brides, two homegrown grooms, and a guest list of nearly the entire population of the town of Fairfield.

Anne and Matt preceded the other couple away from the arbor where the ceremony had been held, down the white carpeted walk to the area where they would form a receiving line to greet their guests. As they waited for the other couple, they had a moment to whisper endearments.

"Darling," Matt said. "I know how important your house is to you and I promise you now that I will do my best to see that you can always live here."

"Not my house, our house," she corrected him, as Janet and Bill arrived to join them and guests began to rise from the sea of folding chairs which filled the yard.

"My house, too!" Karen said, tugging at Anne's arm in order to be noticed.

"Of course, Sweetheart, this house is going to be home to *all* of us." Anne told her, stooping down to look into the serious eyes of the small child, adorable in her flower girl dress of crisp white lace trimmed with ribbons of palest green and gold. She gave the child a warm, loving hug, her heart filled with joy that she was to serve as a mother to the perfect little creature.

"And perhaps there's even room for a few more," Matt hinted with a grin.

"Absolutely!" Anne replied, rising to her feet and lifting her face for a kiss from her new husband, a man she knew would be a wonderful father to any child who might come their way.

# ABOUT THE AUTHOR

Betty Killebrew, The author of *Legacy of Love,* is from Clinton, Indiana where she had a long career as a bookkeeper at the local newspaper office before semi-retiring and changing to a part-time position as a proofreader. Being so close to the publishing world encouraged her to launch her own quarterly magazine where she honed her skills as a writer over its twelve years of publication. During her tenure as publisher, she authored numerous short stories and human interest columns.

Several years ago, she ceased publishing her magazine to focus on writing novels. She is the author of two other books, *Love Poems with a Story*, and *The Life and Adventures of Jonathan Cat.* Another book is in the works.

**Author's contact information:**
Betty L. Killebrew
1110 W. 3rd
Clinton, IN 47842